ARIEL TACHNA

Contemporary Romance at its Finest

Her Two Dads

"…one of the most emotionally rewarding and uplifting love stories that I have read in a long time." —Dark Diva Reviews

"This is one of the best books I have ever read." —Judging the Book by Its Pages

"…a fast-paced story with a well developed storyline that will leave you begging for more. It's a story about overcoming hatred and bigotry, the joys of parenthood and discovering love when you least expect it." —Literary Nymphs

"…a sweet and stirring novel about the power of love and family." —Romance Junkies

Seducing C.C.

"…a great comfort read." —Blackraven Reviews

"…a seductively sexy and romantic story." —Night Owl Reviews

Out of the Fire

"This story tore at my heart." —TwoLips Recommended Read

"…something in it for just about everybody who has a kink…" —The Romance Studio

http://www.dreamspinnerpress.com

Once in a
LIFETIME

—

ARIEL TACHNA

Dreamspinner Press

Published by
Dreamspinner Press
4760 Preston Road
Suite 244-149
Frisco, TX 75034
http://www.dreamspinnerpress.com/

Once in a Lifetime

Cover Art by Catt Ford

ISBN: 978-1-61372-050-9

Printed in the United States of America
First Edition
July 2011

eBook edition available
eBook ISBN: 978-1-61372-051-6

To the Sourieau family,
who welcomed me with open arms
and still call me their American daughter
nineteen years later

et au Prince Charmant
qui me rend la vie heureuse.

Friday, June 21

I probably should have written that in French. I probably should be writing all of this in French, but this is still my personal journal, and English is still my native language, even if I've worked my butt off over the past year to get my French to a level that will let me live and work in Grenoble for a year.

It's really here. I'm having a little trouble believing it, to tell the truth. When Dr. Kasinski first mentioned his collaboration with Dr. Besson and how he hoped to send one of his students to France, I never thought I'd be the one selected. I worked for it, but I didn't really think it would pay off. I mean, I'm a bio major, not a French student, despite the six semesters I've taken, but it turns out Dr. Besson was impressed enough with my résumé that he accepted me even with my less-than-perfect linguistic skills.

He did, though, and he's done more than I could have imagined to make everything come together. The paperwork went through in record time, I have a place to live for the year with a nice family who has a son close to my age at the local university, he got a hotel room for me in Paris for tomorrow night so I can sleep before I have to take the train, and I have the train ticket in my bag. I'm almost afraid to meet the man in person because I'll end up babbling my gratitude until he fires me to get me to shut up.

At least I know I won't miss my flight. Mom thinks I'm crazy, getting here three hours early, but I'd rather sit in the airport than risk missing my flight. I've got about an hour left until we start boarding. I thought about going to the bar and getting something to drink, just because I can, but I don't like beer, I don't know anything about wine (the French are going to think I'm such an ignorant American, but there's nothing I can do about it since alcohol was strictly prohibited on campus and drinking off campus was a violation of the Honor Code), and mixed drinks give me a headache, so I'll just have to sit here and write in this journal.

Here, where I can be honest with myself because no one else will ever see it, I can admit to being scared to death. I'm a small-town kid from East Texas who went to a conservative Christian college. I'm a barely out of the closet gay man with no idea what to do about it. I'm so out of my league here. Everyone keeps telling me this is a once-in-a-lifetime opportunity, and they're right. They're <u>so</u> right. It's why I'm sitting here in the Dallas airport despite the churning in my stomach. I just wish we'd start boarding so I could feel like I was doing something. Yes, I know, I said I'd rather be here early than miss my flight, but that doesn't mean I like waiting.

I am totally rambling here, which I guess is okay since the idea is to record my thoughts about this whole year as it happens, but I think maybe I'll go for a walk around the airport. It's a long flight to Paris. Stretching my legs now is a probably a good idea.

I'm back. Not sure my nerves are any better, but at least I got some exercise. I'll be glad of that when we're halfway across the Atlantic. The other really cool thing? I heard a boarding announcement for a flight to Montreal in French and then in English, and I understood the French announcement even without hearing the English one! Maybe I won't be as hopeless when I get over there as I thought I would be.

I know I won't fool anyone into thinking I'm French, but on a flight to Paris, the stewardesses should speak French, so maybe I'll try out my skills on them too. Sort of get my feet wet slowly before I get thrown in the deep end. You hear these stories, you know? About how the French all speak English, but they refuse to admit it because they don't like Americans. My French professors told me that's a pile of shit (well, not in those words, since cursing was as forbidden on campus as alcohol), that if I was polite and made an effort, people would respond even if I made mistakes, but I can't help being nervous.

I'm taking a huge risk, deferring admission to Baylor's PhD program for a year to work in France. It's a calculated risk. The experience I'll get with Dr. Besson should give me a leg up on the work I'll have to do as a grad student and eventually as a researcher myself, but if I don't get some good results out of it, enough to get a good recommendation anyway, I could lose my place at Baylor. I guess if that happens, I can apply somewhere less prestigious, but it wouldn't be the same. Not when I've had my heart set on Baylor since I decided I wanted to do basic science research. I mean, I'd be crazy to pass up the chance to study with the likes of Huda Zoghbi or Hugo Bellen. Then again, speaking French might be an advantage with Dr. Bellen, since he's from Belgium.

Okay, I'm rambling again. Or maybe not so much rambling as avoiding the subject. I mean, it's one thing to worry now about the risk, but I've already decided to take it, and it's way too late to second-guess myself. I get on the plane in about twenty minutes. I've already shipped my books and a box of winter clothes. The Moreaus are expecting me the day after tomorrow, and Dr. Besson expects me at work on Wednesday. It's easier to worry about the long-term risk than it is to think about what tomorrow or next week might bring, to think about what I've promised myself for this year.

No more hiding. No more burying myself in work so I don't have to search for an excuse to get out of this event or that date where everyone will expect me to be as interested in the girls as all the other guys. I'm not interested in girls. Period. End of discussion. This year is my gift to myself. My chance to figure out who I am and what that means. Next year I'll buckle down and get on with the rest of my life. This year is for me. A year to be me, whatever I decide that means.

Now if I only had some idea how to go about that. How exactly does one go about being open about being gay without being a drag queen or a complete fairy or any of the other stereotypes that aren't me at all?

I have no idea how to answer that question, but I'm hoping I can figure it out. Otherwise there's not a whole lot of point in going somewhere so far away for a year.

They're calling my flight. Time to pack this up for now. I'm sure I'll write more on the plane.

How cool is this? I'm sitting next to this older French lady. She speaks about ten words of English, from what I can tell, but she's totally willing to talk to me. Even better, she can understand me! I mean, I've seen her smile a few times like something I said was quaint or reminded her of her kids when they were first learning to talk, but she can understand me. I'm talking to a random French person and she can understand me. If we weren't stuck on the plane, I'd be doing the Snoopy dance for sure.

She started simply by greeting me, easy enough. So I replied and asked her how she was doing. She looked charmed, so I didn't pull my journal back out right away or put my headphones on or do any of the things I usually do on a plane to guarantee my seatmate leaves me alone. She asked if I was going to France for business or pleasure. I told her both. She looked like she wasn't sure I'd really understood her question, so I explained about the job and Grenoble and living in France for a year. I was surprised by how much I could say. I mean, I've studied technical terms to be able to talk to the other lab techs and to Dr. Besson, but I was actually able to explain that I would be doing research in a lab for a doctor who studies sickle-cell anemia. I didn't get into the technical stuff because some of it is confidential, but I could at least give her the general idea. It turns out she's from Annecy, which isn't all that far from Grenoble, so she told me all about the region and things to do and try. I won't remember them all, I'm sure, but I can remember she said I should give Lyon a try (but not the andouillette sausage) and that for skiing, I should skip Chamonix and go straight to Courchevel, but for the beaches, I should avoid Provence altogether and go west of the Rhone to Languedoc.

God, I can't believe how much we were able to discuss! And the stewardess came by with drinks while we were talking and didn't bat an eye when I ordered in French. Maybe I'm not as hopeless as I was afraid I'd be.

Maybe I really can do this. And if I can handle the language barrier this easily, maybe the rest won't be as hard as I thought it would either.

Saturday, June 22

I don't think I've ever been so tired in my life. It's only noon here in Paris, but that's five a.m. at home and on next to no sleep. I couldn't get comfortable on the plane even though the seats were better than a lot of planes I've been on. The hotel in Paris let me leave my bags with the concierge, but I can't actually get in the room until after three. I'd kill for a nap right now, but instead I'm sitting in a sidewalk café across from the hotel hoping the caffeine in this coffee will keep me upright until three.

The coffee is amazing. I mean, I thought I knew something about coffee, having survived college, but this… "plain" black coffee has never tasted so good. It's rich and strong without being thick or bitter. I don't know if it's this café or if it's French coffee in general, but I may never look at Starbucks the same again.

I know I ought to go for a walk, see part of the city or something, but my legs feel like lead. I'll order lunch in a few minutes and hope that helps wake me up. I don't know what's going on today, but the street here is blocked like they're going to have a parade or a demonstration or something. I just hope it doesn't last very long, although as tired as I am, I could probably sleep through the noise. Maybe the waiter will know what's going on. I'll ask him when he brings my lunch. Steak-frites. I'm such a tourist, but I needed something more substantial than a sandwich after the croissant they called breakfast on the plane. Another one of those things I know I'll have to get used to. No full American breakfast around here, just a couple of croissants or a baguette and jelly, or if I'm lucky, a bowl of cereal. Once I get to Grenoble and start working, I can always buy my own box of cereal if the Moreaus go the more traditional route for breakfast, but until that first paycheck is in the bank, I'm hoarding every penny I can. Dr. Besson warned me to bring enough money for two months on the off chance there was a problem with my paperwork. I hope it won't come to that, but if it does, I don't intend to be caught short. I have to pay the Moreaus for room and board, I have to be able to pay for either the tramway or the bus to get to work (still have to figure that one out, but I'm hoping I can do that tomorrow when I get to town), and I have to get lunch for myself. That doesn't sound like a lot, but I'd rather not go hungry, so I'll pinch pennies until then. At least I won't have to worry about a car, though. And here's lunch.

Oh my God! You'll never believe what the waiter just told me when I asked about the blocked streets. He said today is Paris's Gay Pride parade, and that it will pass through here in a couple of hours. I want to see it, but a part of me is screaming at me to run away and hide in my hotel room. I won't do that, though. I won't let myself be that person any more. Granted, I didn't expect it to happen this fast, but I came to France with the idea of finding myself as a gay man, and suddenly here's my chance to start. I'll watch the parade, maybe see if there are fliers for clubs or something. Not that I'll be living in Paris, but there's nothing to stop me from coming up for a weekend once I get settled in. It's a three-hour train ride if I take the TGV direct, and not all that much more if I have to change trains in Lyon.

I'm eating as I write, and I can't believe how good the food is. It's a steak with french fries. This is not supposed to be "rock my world" food. One of my professors told me I hadn't eaten until I'd been to France, but I didn't believe her. Maybe I should have listened a little more carefully. I wonder what else she told me that I discounted too soon. I suppose I'll find out. I've got half an hour until the Pride parade is supposed to start, so I'd better eat quickly. I'm nervous, yes, but I don't want to miss a second of it. I'm afraid if I do, I'll lose my nerve.

Sunday, June 23

You know how I said yesterday that I'd never been so tired in my life? Yeah, well, I lied. Now I've never been so tired in my life. I'm on the train to Grenoble with all my bags, trying to make myself stay awake. Not that I think anyone is going to rifle through my suitcases if I sleep, but I have to get this down before I lose all my impressions.

The Gay Pride parade yesterday was unlike anything I've ever seen before. There were thousands of people there. Hundreds of thousands for all I know, although that's probably an exaggeration. The streets were packed, people climbing on top of bus stops and newspaper stands so they could see, all up in the trees and on lamp posts. And these were just the people who'd come out to <u>see</u> the parade. The people actually in the parade were even more unbelievable, but I'll get to that in a minute.

The parade passed in front of my hotel, but it didn't actually start there, so I had a little longer to eat lunch than I'd thought I would (which was good because the food was too amazing to rush, and the dessert was even better. Crème caramel... I think I'm in love). When I finished eating, I went outside to see what was going on or what I could see. The parade hadn't reached us yet (it starts down in Montparnasse, the people around me said), but the party had already started. I've never seen anything like it. Yes, I know, I already said that, but it bears repeating. All around me, people were holding hands and kissing. Not making out, but leaning over and kissing their boyfriends or girlfriends like it was the most normal thing in the world. I guess for them it is. They're out and in a relationship with someone they care about. For them, it's no different than the straight couples I knew in college who didn't think anything of kissing each other goodbye or hello. This is just the first time I've seen gay couples do it.

The first time, I caught myself looking away, like there was something shameful in what they were doing. I hate that reaction in myself. The only difference between them and me is that they got up the courage to come out some time ago, and I'm just doing it now. Then I noticed something. Nobody else looked away. Nobody else cared. Even the straight couples in the crowd. There wasn't anything shameful in those kisses or the clasped hands. Not here.

I'm not naïve. Well, not that naïve. I know there will still be people who might not approve, but this isn't East Texas. I don't have to hide who I am here. If I learned one thing yesterday (and I learned a whole lot more than one thing!), it was that. It really is okay to be myself and to be gay.

There's something incredibly freeing about writing those words. It's okay to be myself and to be gay. Maybe I'll write them a few more times until I'm sure they've completely sunk in.

It's okay to be gay.

So anyway, there's this huge party atmosphere already, music playing from somewhere, maybe one of the cafés, maybe someone had a radio. I couldn't ever decide where it was coming from at that point. Later, once we got to place de la Bastille, it was from the soundstage, of course, but that was different. This wasn't anything organized as far as I could tell, more a matter of the giddiness spilling out of everyone. People were dancing, right there on the sidewalks, as they waited for the parade to arrive.

When it did, it was a revelation. I saw drag queens and leather guys. I saw people of every ethnicity in traditional dress, sometimes cross-dressing, sometimes not. And the colors! Everything was so bright. I swear, the sun shone brighter as the parade approached. How could it not? It was such a celebration of life and love and diversity. I can't even imagine what my friends from college would think, but I'm done with that. It doesn't matter what they would think because I know what I think. I think what I saw yesterday in the streets of Paris is the way life should be. Not the parade or the party, although that was fantastic. The celebration of diversity in all the senses of the word. That's the way life should be. That's the way my life will be.

Because for every drag queen or leather guy I saw, I saw fifty, no, a hundred people just like me. People in street clothes, celebrating their right to be different. I saw a soccer team that had as their motto "gay and straight, the team that defends diversity." I can't even begin to imagine something like that at home. In San Francisco, maybe, but I don't live in San Francisco. I got so caught up in the joie de vivre that I forgot all about being tired. I followed the parade through half of Paris, it felt like, until we reached place de la Bastille and the dance party. My legs felt like rubber by the time I got there, but the energy in the air was catching. I feel it today, though!

The music wasn't anything I was familiar with, but it didn't matter. Everyone was so caught up in it, dancing right there in the place, which was completely blocked off. I don't think I've ever danced so much or with so many people before. Every time I'd stop to catch my breath, someone else would grab my hand and pull me back into the dancing. Men, women, it didn't matter. Somehow I don't think my friends at home had this in mind when they talked about the once-in-a-lifetime experience. Then again, maybe it won't be once in a lifetime. Maybe I'll make this my annual pilgrimage. I'll come to Paris every year for Pride and dance in the streets until I'm too old to dance.

At some point the party spilled out of place de la Bastille into the Marais, which I learned is very queer friendly, although yesterday, at least, all of Paris seemed queer friendly. It does give me an idea of where to hang out if I come back for a weekend, though, so I made a mental note of it last night and I'm writing it down now. I ate dinner at some point last night, although by then I was so exhausted I couldn't tell you what I ate, but I couldn't tear myself away from the joyousness of the evening either: the dancing, the music, the everything that made the entire day so unique. The minute I came out of the restaurant, I got pulled back into the crowd again.

When I finally stumbled back to the hotel a little before midnight, I barely got my shoes off before collapsing onto the bed and falling asleep. Fortunately my train didn't leave until almost two today or I'd have missed it for sure. By four thirty, I'll be in Grenoble. Madame Moreau said she'd meet me at the train station. I feel kind of bad making her come get me, but honestly, as tired as I am, I don't think I'd trust myself to navigate the bus system today. I have Monday and Tuesday to take care of stuff like setting up a bank account and taking my passport to the prefecture to get the temporary work visa replaced with the official one. I can figure out the buses and trams then.

I fell asleep on the train, pen in hand. Fortunately the TGV is a direct train with just the one stop, so I didn't have to deal with the embarrassment of sleeping through my stop. I found Mme Moreau waiting for me on the platform as promised. She couldn't have been more gracious about my obviously sleep-deprived conversation or the amount of luggage I have. It's not like I'm coming for a weekend. I'm here for the full year. Anyway, she drove me home. And what a home! I had the address, but I was lazy and hadn't bothered to look it up on a map. It's practically on the Esplanade! I look out one window and see the mountains and out the other and see the river. It's freaking unbelievable. And the house itself… First of all, it's a house, which isn't always the case. A lot of families live in apartments rather than free-standing houses, but the Moreaus have a house, and a really nice one too. It's probably a couple hundred years old (even as I write that, my mind boggles) with thick walls and big windows with shutters that actually work. They call them volets apparently. And they close them all every night and open them all again every morning. How cool is that!

Anyway, the Moreaus have three kids, but only two of them live at home full time. Elodie and Serge are both in high school and seem fun. I don't know how much time I'll spend with them, given their school schedule and my work schedule, but they'll be someone to talk to at the dinner table if nothing else. They both seemed excited about having someone to practice their English with, so I agreed to help them with their schoolwork in the fall, as long as they promised to help me with my French. They just finished school for the summer. So did Pierre, the oldest son, but he wasn't here tonight. He has one year left in college, so I'm hoping he'll be willing to show me around a little this summer before classes start back for him, since he's the closest to my age and so the one most likely to know the kinds of places I'd enjoy meeting people.

What else? Oh, my room… it's not anything fancy, but it's nice in its simplicity. It's sort of a loft room, or maybe a converted attic, although the conversion isn't recent. You can see the beams of the roof. These old, heavy wooden… logs. I mean, they've been shaped and all, but they're huge. Like full tree trunks supporting the roof. I've got a bed, a desk, a closet, and my own toilet and sink. I have to go downstairs to shower, but if I have to get up in the middle of the night to take a leak, I don't have to worry about stumbling down the stairs or waking anyone else up. And one whole wall is lined with bookshelves. I haven't looked at any of the books yet, but at least if I get bored, I'll have something to read. Even if they're the classics instead of contemporary fiction, it'll be good for my French.

Mme Moreau gave me a key, which makes sense because I'll need to come and go for work and stuff, but that was it. No reminder of what time I needed to be in. Just a key and a request that if I come in late, to be quiet so I don't wake the family up. As if I'd be that disrespectful, but she doesn't really know me yet, so it's a reasonable request. I'm not quite sure what to do with myself with no curfew. I went from living with my parents and having a ten o'clock curfew on weeknights and midnight on the weekends, to college where curfew ranged from eleven to one thirty. Even when I was home in the summers, my parents expected me home at midnight. During the week, I'm sure I'll be home far earlier than that here too since I'll have to work the next day, but in theory, I could stumble in at four or five in the morning, or, if I met someone I wanted to spend time with, simply not come home one night. I'm not sure if that's liberating or frightening. I never had to worry in college about needing an excuse to leave if a situation got uncomfortable. Even if I wasn't on campus, the local kids knew all about our curfews, so I'd tell them I had to be back for dorm check and that got me out of anything I needed out of. I won't have that here. It sounds like a funny thing to miss when I was just talking about the freedom, but it means I have to make those decisions for myself now instead of having them made for me. One more step into adulthood.

I'm starting to babble again, I know, but I've reached that point beyond exhaustion where sleep is difficult. I was hoping writing some would help me settle for the night, but it hasn't yet. My mind is racing with everything I have to get done tomorrow and on Tuesday, and my stomach is churning because I haven't the slightest idea how to do it. I asked M. Moreau about the bank and he recommended one that has lots of ATMs and no fees, so that much is done. Now I just have to hope my French is up to the process of opening the account. My success on the plane and in Paris notwithstanding, that will be a very different kind of conversation.

This is ridiculous. I'm putting down my pen and going to bed. Otherwise I really won't be able to get everything done tomorrow that I need to do.

Tuesday, June 25

I was bad and didn't write yesterday, but really, there wasn't a whole lot interesting in spending the day doing paperwork. Paperwork at the bank, paperwork at the prefecture, paperwork at CAF. The good news is I have a bank account, I have a work visa (no delays in getting my salary processed! Woohoo!), and I might actually get a subsidy on my rent. Another one of those things I had no idea about. Because the CNRS is a government-funded agency, I'm technically a government employee, and so I'm covered by health insurance and eligible for certain social benefits. I could get to like it over here.

That's the boring stuff. Tonight was much more interesting. Pierre—the Moreaus' oldest son—came home for dinner. I'd been thinking of him as being a year younger than me, but he's really not. His birthday is tomorrow—he'll be twenty-two too—and he invited me to the party on Saturday. Not the family party, but the one afterward with all his friends from the university. I mean, he invited me to the family party too, but that one isn't nearly as interesting to me as the other one. A chance to meet Pierre's friends, people more or less my age who might become my friends.

I'm kind of hesitant to admit it, even here in my journal where no one else will see it, but Pierre is kinda cute. Who am I kidding? He's really cute. That's silly and pointless because even if he's single (and I don't know that he is), he's probably straight. And supposing I got lucky and he was gay, there's no chance he'd be interested in me. I mean, I'm just here for a year, and then I'm going home. Not a whole lot of future in that for either of us. It didn't stop me from looking, though. He's got sandy brown hair that curls all over the place, and these gorgeous brown eyes that danced with excitement the whole time we talked about the party on Saturday. The family one is a late lunch, probably a huge meal if what everyone told me is true, and then the one with his friends is in a club later that evening. L'Absolu, I think he said the name was. He said we could go together from the family party to the other one, so I don't actually have to worry about finding it myself.

He also said, to his mother, not to me, that since classes were out for the summer, he'd probably be home for dinner a lot more often. Maybe… maybe I can get some other invitations to parties and stuff with him around. I want to make friends, to have a life while I'm here, and I think Pierre and I could be friends. We have a lot of things in common, we discovered at dinner. We like a lot of the same movies and music, although he mentioned some French artists I'm not familiar with. He said he'd lend me some CDs so I can give them a try. I was a little embarrassed, honestly. He knows so much about American music, and I know so little about French music, but that didn't seem to bother him.

Is this what a crush feels like? That's a stupid question, I know, but I never let myself even think about it in college. Besides being strictly forbidden, I wasn't ready to admit who I was. Not there, anyway. I had fantasy guys, actors and stuff I thought were cute, but that's not the same thing. Pierre's a real person. I mean, he's someone I actually know and can hang out with as opposed to some publicist's creation who I ever only see in staged interviews or on the big screen.

My stomach is all tied in knots and my mind keeps replaying our conversation from dinner. Pierre actually complimented my French. I couldn't believe it. He said he didn't have any trouble understanding me. I got an intellectual thrill when I could talk to the lady on the plane and the guy at the bank, but this was a thrill on a different level. That's what makes me think this is a crush.

Oh, here's Pierre with the CDs.

How do you know if a guy is flirting with you?

Pierre came up to my room after dinner, while I was writing earlier, and brought a whole stack of CDs. That was already pretty cool, but then he stayed to chat, perched on the edge of my bed while I sat at my desk, my closed journal on my knees like some kind of stupid security blanket. He went through all the CDs with me, telling me who all the artists were again and why he liked different songs and styles. It was interesting and fun and I'm glad he came upstairs, but I got this feeling he was looking for something more. He didn't say anything, obviously, or I wouldn't be asking the question, but it seemed like he met my eyes constantly and that he sat just a little more splay-legged than comfortable, like he wanted me to look at him, and then he'd lean forward whenever I said anything (which wasn't often because I was afraid I'd say the wrong thing once the thought popped into my head that he might be flirting), like he was hanging on every word I said.

He didn't agree with everything I said when I did manage to say something. He still doesn't like Keith Urban, but I guess country music is an acquired taste if you don't grow up with it like I did. Dad doesn't think much of him either, despite having grown up in the country.

If we were at home and if Pierre were a girl, or I were, I'd be pretty sure he was flirting at least lightly, but everything is so different here that I'm afraid to judge anything by what I knew at home. Maybe everything tonight was perfectly normal for him and another French guy (or girl) wouldn't have thought anything of it. I guess that's the first drawback of trying to figure out how to be gay in a culture other than my own. I don't know the mores here well enough yet to know what's French and what's gay.

I start work tomorrow (on a completely different note). I figured out the buses and the times today. As long as the buses run on time, I can make it in less than half an hour. For the summer, I might even see about finding a bike I could use, because given where the buses run, I bet I could get there as fast or faster on a bike. The road up to the house is steep, but the rest of the city is surprisingly flat for being so close to the Alps.

That's a problem for this weekend. I'm certainly not going to find a bike between tonight and tomorrow morning.

Wednesday, June 26

I started work today. It's not going to be anything like working in Dr. Kasinski's lab. Not that the work he's doing isn't good work, because it is, but that's a college lab. This is… this is the big time.

Everyone was friendly, if a little reserved—which I think is typical of the French actually. They're polite but not effusive until you get to know them a little better. And they were very amused at my tie. *sigh* Another one of those things I'll have to get used to. I'm used to wearing a tie pretty much all the time. Not on weekends, but we had to wear them to class, to chapel, to lunch… if we were out of the dorm for anything other than Phys Ed before five in the evening, we pretty much had a tie on. That isn't the case here. Everyone was very professional in their behavior and their attitudes, but not in their dress. I asked Jean-Mathias, the tech at the bench next to mine, about it, and he said with all the chemicals we work with, it's easy to ruin clothes, and so people tend to go for comfortable rather than fancy at work.

I always wore a lab coat in Dr. Kasinski's lab to avoid that since I didn't have a choice. I'll have to rethink my clothing options for the rest of the year. I packed all my shirts and ties thinking I'd need them for work and not nearly as many of my T-shirts and sweatshirts thinking I'd only need them on the weekend. Maybe Mom would ship me some, and I can always buy a few here. Mme Moreau told me tonight at dinner that I should do laundry whenever I need to. She said she'd show me how for the first load, but after that, not to feel like she needed to be around. Fais comme chez toi has definitely been the motto since I got here. Make yourself at home would be the English equivalent, I guess, although the words don't match up. That's one of the things I love about language. The way different languages get across the same idea but with totally different words.

I'm digressing, although I guess if I'm allowed to digress anywhere, it's here.

So, work…

Today was mostly orientation. Figuring out where everything is, who everyone is, what my part in the big project will be, making sure I had all the paperwork filed with the CNRS so I can get paid on time. Dr. Besson said it looked like everything was in order and that my first paycheck should arrive on time at the end of July. He also said I should be covered by health insurance starting on July 1, which is just a couple of days away. That's a relief, because even though I'm still on my parents' insurance for a few more months, I'd hate to think of the complications of trying to get medical treatment approved all the way over here. Not that I expect to need it, but it's nice to know I'll have it in case I get sick.

The highlight of my day, though, was lunch with Jean-Mathias. (Is that bad?) He just finished his graduate work in biology and started working in Dr. Besson's lab about a year ago. I guess the American equivalent would be post-doc, but I don't think that translates here. He isn't studying or training, from what I could tell. This is his job now, the start of his career. If things go well for him in Dr. Besson's lab, he could apply for grants in a few years to start his own lab, or he could stay where he is and do bench work. He said he doesn't know which he'd prefer yet. I can understand that. If I had the choice of a real career, salary wise, without having to fight for grants, I'd take it. That's the one part of my future I'm not looking forward to.

I really enjoyed our conversation. Jean-Mathias is a couple of years older than me and a real sports enthusiast. He was talking about going biking up in the mountains this weekend. I think of myself as being in pretty good shape, but I'm not sure I'd want to tackle the mountains yet. But he also plays soccer and some basketball and mentioned swimming. I obviously can't make plans for this weekend since I have Pierre's parties on Saturday, but I'm hoping Jean-Mathias wouldn't mind me tagging along when he goes biking or whatever. After four years of having a Phys Ed class every semester, I've gotten used to being active. I don't want to lose that simply because there's no longer a professor checking my BMI at the end of the semester as part of my grade. I've seen what obesity does to people—my town isn't known for healthy eating—and I don't want that to happen to me.

It's kind of cool. I've been here less than a week, and I've already made two friends. Or at least I've met two people who could be my friends with a little time and effort. I have time and I'm willing to make the effort. This is going to be a good year.

Oh, the other thing I did today was pick up an adapter for my laptop, so I'll have Internet access now. The Moreaus have a wireless connection and don't mind me using it, so maybe I'll search the 'net for a gay club or to see if Grenoble has a pride parade like the one in Paris. It would be fun to do another parade, but I'm far more interested in making the connection with other people in the community. If I'm going to explore that side of me, I have to find people who can guide me. I'll still do things with Pierre and Jean-Mathias, if they're willing, of course. There's more to me than being gay, and the last thing I want is to lose out on friendships. Obviously if I'm looking for a boyfriend, he has to be gay, but I can be friends with anyone.

Mme Moreau is calling everyone for dinner. I have no idea what we're having, but I've been smelling it since I got home, so I'm sure it will be delicious.

Since today was Pierre's birthday, even though the party is on Saturday, Mme Moreau made all his favorite dishes for dinner. We had charcuterie as an appetizer, duck with cherries, and then salad, of course, and this melon that's sort of like a cantaloupe, only not quite, with port wine for dessert. And we had wine with dinner. I wasn't sure I'd like it. I've never developed a taste for beer or been exposed to much alcohol of any other variety, but it was really good. It was from M. Moreau's brother's vineyard. I didn't know they had a vintner in the family.

They asked me how I liked the wine, of course, and I had to confess my absolute ignorance, although I did assure them I really enjoyed what was in my glass. Pierre, Serge, and Elodie couldn't believe I'd never had wine before. I tried to explain that I went to a conservative Christian university, but while I know they understood my words, the concept is too foreign to them. Universities here are public institutions, and France's definition of the separation of church and state goes a lot farther than ours. For me, it means no state-defined religion. Here, it means no religion in any public domain. I keep bumping up against these differences that surprise me. I don't know that it will really change all that much in my daily life. I can go to church on Sunday. I can be involved in any church group I want to be. It's just a different attitude.

So anyway, I explained about the Honor Code to the best of my ability, and they promised to take me to their uncle's some weekend soon to expand my education. It's odd to think that these teenagers of fifteen and seventeen know more about wine than I do, but when I said that, they reminded me that France doesn't have a drinking age. A purchasing age, but not a drinking age. Kids here grow up drinking watered-down wine on special occasions, and as they get older, that becomes regular wine on special occasions. Plus, they hear their parents talk about it, so even when they don't taste the wine, they learn the vernacular. Pierre and his parents each had a couple of glasses, but Serge and Elodie only had one each, and it wasn't even a full glass, so it's not like they're out getting drunk.

It's a different mindset than what I'm used to, but I wonder, in a way, if it isn't a more responsible one. There's no mystery so there's no reason to run off to college (well, most colleges) and engage in the typical freshmen binges. Not that we had that, but I have friends from high school who came home after their first semester and all they could talk about were the parties and getting drunk all the time.

Speaking of drunk, I think the wine must have gone to my head even more than I realized because I'm having a hard time keeping this coherent. So, to try to finish my tale, the whole discussion led to me admitting I'd like to know more. I doubt I'll ever be a connoisseur, but I'd like to be conversant anyway. I'd like to know what to order with what so if I'm out with friends (or a date), I don't end up looking like an idiot. Pierre immediately offered to take me to some wine tastings in town and out to his uncle's house some weekend so I could have the grand tour. And so now I'm back to wondering if he's flirting with me again. Serge and Elodie are too young to go with us to a store because you pay for the wine tasting, which constitutes purchasing wine, but they immediately asked to come to their uncle's as well. Pierre didn't exactly say no, but it seemed like he didn't want them to join us. I don't mind if they come, honestly, but I kind of like the idea of spending the weekend alone with Pierre. Maybe if I plan a trip some weekend to visit some of the places the lady on the plane told me about, I can see if he'd like to come along.

Of course I'm probably wrong, and he's not flirting, and any trip, to his uncle's or otherwise, will just be a weekend as friends. I need to set up my computer and find out more about Grenoble's gay community. Then I can stop worrying about Pierre except as a friend.

That's what I'll do tomorrow as soon as I get home from work. I'll be awake enough (and sober enough) then to get everything working right. I'd be almost afraid to try tonight. I might break something. I'm not as recovered from the jet lag as I thought, and the wine didn't help. Time for bed.

Friday, June 28

Yes, I know, I skipped a day again, but other than having lunch with Jean-Mathias both yesterday and today, nothing all that interesting has happened, and I don't really want to write just for the sake of writing. I want this journal to mean something later on. I want to be able to read it with interest instead of rolling my eyes at another entry that says, "Went to work today. Came home, had dinner and went to bed."

Jean-Mathias asked me at lunch today if I wanted to go biking with him and some of his buddies on Saturday. I'd like to. I think it sounds fun, but I told him it'll have to wait for another weekend since I have the party on Saturday. He was very understanding and told me to have fun and not drink too much. I assured him not to worry about that. It's not like I'm much of a drinker at all, much less a heavy drinker. I have no interest in getting falling down drunk.

When I said that, well, not exactly that since I don't know the equivalent expression in French, but when I told him I wasn't planning on getting drunk, he asked if I wanted to join a pickup soccer game Sunday afternoon. Soccer isn't my best sport, but I know how to play, so I agreed.

We're meeting at three on Sunday at a field on the south side of town. Jean-Mathias gave me the address and the tramway stop. I should be able to find it with that. So now I have all kinds of plans for this weekend. And here I was worried I wouldn't find anything to do in my spare time.

I'm excited about the party tomorrow. I asked Pierre what I should wear since I obviously misjudged work attire. He said a nice shirt and slacks would be fine, no tie required, and that we could change before we went out to the club. I'm not sure what I'd change into since I don't exactly have anything I'd consider clubbing clothes, but I'll figure something out. Or I'll wear the slacks and shirt and hope Pierre's friends don't mind too much. I am who I am, after all, and if they can't appreciate that, I wouldn't want them as friends anyway.

The family party tomorrow is at Pierre's grandmother's house. I should go out in the morning and get flowers for her. Even if I'm coming as part of the family, I'm still a guest and it'll be the first time I meet her. Hopefully she'll appreciate a gesture like that. Another one of those things my professors said: never visit someone's house empty-handed. I brought gifts from home for the Moreaus, but I didn't know I'd be visiting the grandmother so soon. Otherwise I'd have brought something for her too.

I don't expect I'll feel like writing tomorrow night when we get back from the club, but I'll write on Sunday before or after church (depending on what time I wake up). Mass is at 10:30, which isn't too early, so I might wake up in time to write beforehand. If not, I'll be home by noon, which still gives me two and a half hours before I need to leave to meet Jean-Mathias and his friends at the soccer field.

I also got online tonight and did some searching. I found an organization called Cigale. Well, C.I.Ga.Le to be precise, the Collectif Interassocations Gays et Lesbiennes, but it's sort of a clearinghouse for GLBT organizations in the region. The web site has links to several different groups, some more targeted than others. They all look interesting, but the one that really caught my attention is a group called David et Jonathan. It's a Christian GLBT group. They meet once a month, the first Wednesday of the month actually. That's next week. I have no idea what I'd bring to the potluck dinner, but I suppose I could get a dessert from the pâtisserie or else throw together a salad. I'm nervous, but I think this would be a really good first step for me, a way to balance my faith and my sexuality. And if I go and it's an absolute disaster, I don't have to go back next month. First, though, I have two parties tomorrow and a soccer game on Sunday. I'll worry about the potluck next week.

Sunday, June 30

Wow, um, I have no idea where to start this today.

You know all those questions about whether Pierre was flirting with me? I'm pretty sure the answer is yes, but that's getting ahead of the story. Let me see if I can start at the beginning and make this make sense.

Pierre's parties were yesterday. I managed to find a florist and buy flowers for Pierre's grandmother, who seemed touched that I'd thought of her since the gathering was in Pierre's honor, not hers. I was right about the food. We had eight different courses, all of them amazing. These crusty little toast squares with paté on them to start, and then the appetizer, which was fresh tomatoes with a mustard vinaigrette. French onion soup, some kind of fish in a cream sauce, braised rabbit with these tiny little green beans that don't taste anything like my mother's beans (thank goodness!), salad, a cheese course, and then dessert. Of course, the meal lasted four hours, so it's not like we ate in a rush, and the portions were small, but it was still a lot of food. And a lot of wine. A white wine up through the fish course, then a red wine with the rabbit, salad, and cheese, and then this sort of golden wine with dessert. I didn't catch the name of any of them, but I did meet Pierre's uncle Hugues, the vintner, and he said we'd be welcome to come visit any weekend, and that if I wanted to help with the harvest in the fall, he'd be glad of another pair of hands.

I met the other uncles and aunts, too, and a bunch of the cousins. I'm not sure I met all of them, but enough I can't remember everyone's names, so I'm not even going to try. There was one rather odd conversation, though. I met one of the older cousins, my age or a little older. I think her name was Patricia. Anyway, she kept watching me oddly until Mme Moreau introduced me, but it was her comment that threw me. She said, "Oh, you're the American lodger. I wondered why Pierre brought a copain to the family party." At the time, I shrugged it off, although it didn't really explain the odd look on her face. Copain means friend, buddy.

Except it can also mean boyfriend.

I think she thought I was Pierre's boyfriend before we were introduced. I'm not exactly sure how I feel about that, but let me finish the story first.

When that party ended, we all came back to the house so Pierre could change before we went out. I switched my slacks out for a pair of jeans but left my dress shirt on because I didn't really want to wear a T-shirt and I don't have anything in between as far as formality is concerned. Shopping is definitely on my list of things to do once my first paycheck hits the bank. Pierre fussed around me a bit, untucking my shirt and unbuttoning a couple of buttons, insisting I'd be much more comfortable at the club that way. I'm not sure I was more comfortable, but I did fit in a little better than I would have with my shirt tucked in and all buttoned up.

We took the bus to L'Absolu. The buses stop running around eight-thirty on Saturday, but Pierre said we'd take a cab home. He didn't want to worry about parking or about how much he drank. I offered to be the designated driver since I'm not much of a drinker anyway, but that didn't take care of parking, so we took the bus. Once we got to the club, I saw his point. There really wasn't any convenient parking, and there were already cars parked in what few spaces there were.

So, you remember how I said I was going to get online and find the gay-friendly clubs in town? I don't have to do that now. L'Absolu is a gay club. Not that everyone there was gay, because several of Pierre's friends were straight couples, but it was pretty obviously a gay club.

That was odd enough. I mean, I'm not offended or anything. That would be both hypocritical and counterproductive. And I'm not shocked exactly. Pierre didn't disappear into a back room or the restroom or anything for a quickie, nor did any of his friends that I could see, although some of the other people in the club did. It's more that I was unprepared for it. Unprepared for the pure carnality of some of the dancing. Unprepared for my reaction to it. The dancing in Paris at the pride festival was exuberant, giddy, playful, joyful. Random strangers celebrating diversity together. This was far more intent… intense. The couples dancing at the club last night weren't dancing to celebrate diversity. They were dancing to get each other worked up. And watching them had the same effect on me.

Everything about the evening was intended to be enticing. The low lights, the sultry beat of the music, the press of bodies, the heat…. The club had fans going, but like most places in France, it wasn't air-conditioned. Half the guys in the club at least had stripped off their shirts. I don't think I've ever seen that much skin outside of a locker room or pool. I kept trying to find somewhere safe to look so I wouldn't end up ogling this guy or that, but there wasn't anywhere safe. If they weren't dancing, they were making out in a booth or a dark corner or chatting up a guy at the bar with the intention of dancing or making out somewhere. I'm pretty sure I stumbled over more than just making out when I went to the restroom, but I didn't look to be sure. There's a limit to what I want to see.

The smell of sweat and sex permeated the air, so powerful, so arousing. I spent the entire evening somewhere between halfway and completely hard, but the one time I tried to go outside for a breath of fresh air and a moment's respite, I found a couple having sex in the alley. Not exactly conducive to getting myself under control.

All of that was disconcerting enough, but I probably would have been okay with it. Uncomfortably aroused, but okay. The part I don't know how to deal with is Pierre. I don't think he really spent all that much more time with me than with any of his other friends, but every time I looked his way, no matter who he was dancing with or talking to, I found him looking back at me. Almost like he was daring me to join him? Except that doesn't make any sense. He'd already invited me to the party. If he wanted me to talk with him or even dance with him, all he had to do was ask. He never did, though, so now I'm even more confused than I was before. He's almost certainly gay (why else would he have picked a gay club? It can't be because of me. He'd made the plans long before I showed up) and he acted all evening like he wanted my attention, but he never made a move beyond that.

Could he be as unsure as I am? He didn't act unsure with his friends or with the other guys in the club, once word got out that it was his birthday. The only time I saw him without a drink in his hand was when he was dancing, but as soon as he came off the dance floor, someone else would press another drink in his hand. *headdesk* This is why it's easier to just avoid relationships altogether. No confusion, no churning in your stomach, no getting yourself worked up over nothing.

Except what if it isn't nothing? What if Pierre really is interested in me, not just as a friend or someone to practice his English with, but as a boyfriend? What do I do then?

I guess the real question is, what do I want? The problem is I don't know. I barely even feel like I know what my choices are. I had a good time last night despite my confusion. Pierre's friends were a lot of fun, and when I wasn't wondering what Pierre was thinking, I danced with some of them, the guys as well as the girls. Maybe that's part of the problem. Pierre saw me dancing with the girls, because why shouldn't I? Girls can be fun. Some of my closest friends in college were girls because they weren't nearly as uncomfortable to be around as the guys were, with the whole gay but not out thing.

If he was watching me, trying to decide if I'm gay, seeing me dancing with the girls might have thrown him off. It's not exactly my style to pull off my shirt and do the bump and grind with anyone, so he probably couldn't see any difference in the way I danced with the girls and the other guys. Just because I felt the difference doesn't mean anyone else noticed.

Dancing with the girls was fun, but dancing with the guys was… somewhere between torture and ecstasy. Ecstasy because I was finally being myself. Torture because I didn't have the right to touch, not really. I came home last night and dreamed all kinds of illicit things. Bodies moving together, rubbing against each other, faster and harder until… well, until things got messy.

I did a lot of praying at church this morning, needless to say. Somehow I don't think any of the things I dreamed about last night would have been allowed under the Honor Code at school. No illicit, unscriptural sexual acts, and all that. Today's readings were on the value of love. Real, powerful, God-given, committed love. And the beauty of that was the priest. He didn't use the word marriage. He used the word committed. Any couple living together in commitment to one another was blessed and a blessing. Maybe I'm reading more into the choice of words than he meant, filtering it through the lens of my own questions and needs, and maybe it's a language issue. Maybe there's an implication I didn't catch implied in the word investir. Maybe, or maybe given what I found on the David et Jonathan web site, there's a school of thought where homosexuality is concerned here that I never encountered at home. I'll see how things go on Wednesday, and I spoke to the priest after Mass. It turns out that in addition to saying Mass at l'église St Louis, he works with the Pole Étudiant Catholique, a college group that also meets on Wednesday nights. I got the address from him, although I'm going to David et Jonathan this week. I could go the other three or four Wednesdays of the month. It'll take the place of chapel.

Mme Moreau just called up to say lunch was ready if I wanted to eat. I'm not entirely sure I'm ready to face Pierre this morning, but that would be churlish and childish. Neither of us did anything wrong. I'm just confused. Okay, lunch now, soccer this afternoon, and then maybe I'll feel a little more settled.

Soccer this afternoon was great. Jean-Mathias was as good as his word and introduced me all around. We played hard, but it wasn't mean-spirited. I mean, there was the usual teasing and razzing you find any time a group of guys get together to play sports, but it was all in good fun. They had a bit of fun at my expense too, which felt good, like I was accepted. Shane apparently sounds like chêne to them, so then they wanted to know if I was built like an oak and all sorts of other bawdy questions. I know I was the color of a tomato—the curse of fair skin—but we all laughed about it, including my blush, and went on with the game. Of course they've nicknamed me Le chêne now. I suppose that's better than Le chien (the dog), which isn't all that different in sound. Shane Le chêne. I'm shaking my head remembering it.

The exercise felt good, though. I haven't had a lot of free time this week to get in any kind of exercise, which is unusual for me after the last four years. Jean-Mathias and his friends invited me back next weekend. I'll definitely take them up on it if nothing else comes up, and I think I'll ask Jean-Mathias tomorrow about finding a bike. Even if I don't ride it to work right away (it is summer and going to get hotter as July and August go on), I can ride it in the evenings or get up early so I can get some exercise, plus maybe I can work up to going riding in the mountains with Jean-Mathias at some point.

Pierre wasn't at lunch or dinner, but nobody seemed surprised by his absence. He must still have his room on campus or at least have somewhere else to stay, because he's only been here about half the time since I arrived. He has his own life. I get that, but it does make last night even more confusing. Oh well. Nothing I can do about it. He'll do what he wants to do, and I'll figure him out, or not, eventually. I do have to say, though, that my first week in France has been a monumental success. I'm pretty sure even in my wildest dreams it didn't go this well.

On the job front, I get to start setting up my first experiments tomorrow now that I've finished all the orientation and safety courses they require of all new employees. Time to see if I really learned as much as I think I did working with Dr. Kasinski. I guess if I get stuck, I can always see if Jean-Mathias will help me out.

Wednesday, July 3

Yes, I know.

Monday, work, lunch with Jean-Mathias, no Pierre.

Tuesday, work, lunch with Jean-Mathias, no Pierre.

There, all caught up.

Work is interesting, and the actual mechanics of it aren't any more complicated than what I was doing in Dr. Kasinski's lab. PCRs, Western or Southern blots, etc. The complicated stuff is the thinking behind it, the science that goes into designing the experiments, but fortunately, while I have to understand the science well enough to carry out the experiments and interpret the data, no one expects me to design the experiments in the first place. Not yet anyway. If that comes later, well, hopefully by later I'll have the experience to not make a complete fool of myself.

Jean-Mathias and I now have "our" table and "our" waiter at the local café where we eat lunch. I'm not sure how that happened so fast, but it did. Not that we'd make anybody get up if someone was already sitting there, obviously. It's nothing like that. It's just the table where we've sat every day for the last week. It's the best table in the café, though. Right by the windows with a view of the street and all the people walking by. When the weather's nice, like it's been this week, they throw the windows open to catch the breeze off the mountains. If it's raining or once it starts to get cold, they'll leave them closed so we still get the view of the people (and the mountains) without being exposed to the elements. The café has sort of an art deco theme going on, very 1920s. Big chandeliers, marble tabletops on wrought iron bases, a big wooden bar, painted ceilings. But despite all of that, it isn't some fancy, stuck-up place. Everyone is very friendly. The waiters wear jeans, and the clientele, at least at lunch time, are mostly people like Jean-Mathias and me. Twenty or thirty something professionals who work at the CNRS or the other nearby offices and businesses, with no time or energy to go home for lunch.

Our waiter is this really cute guy named Paolo. He's from Italy, although he barely has an accent that I can hear. Jean-Mathias might disagree with that since he's actually a native of Grenoble, but I haven't asked. Paolo has already started asking us if we want our usual. I guess we're both a little predictable. Jean-Mathias likes the croque monsieur and I got a goat cheese and herb omelet the first time we went in, and it was so good I haven't even tried anything else. I probably should. If the omelet is that good, maybe everything else is too. I'll surprise Paolo tomorrow by ordering something different.

I stopped by a pâtisserie on the way home and picked up a mille-feuille to take with me to David et Jonathan since I don't really have the means to cook anything. The meal was fun, with lots of different dishes to try. I had no idea what any of them were, but that didn't matter. Definitely delicious. During the meal itself, people mostly got acquainted, shared their week, that kind of thing. Very casual, very low-key. That was nice because it gave me a chance to meet people and get to know them a little. There were only eight of us there, which Alexandre, the leader of the group, said was a little on the small side, but it is summer so people are beginning to take their vacations, even if most people go on vacation in August. Some of the students have gone home for the summer, that sort of thing. He said it's usually more like fifteen to twenty people. I think I'm glad there were only eight last night. I would've been intimidated otherwise. Well, more intimidated than I already was.

It's one thing to write in my journal that I'm gay and that's okay. It's apparently another thing entirely to say it out loud for the first time. I did, though. I looked around the table at the faces of the five men and two women sitting there, and I introduced myself and told them I was gay. I guess it was obvious since I was there, but that didn't seem to matter to the butterflies in my stomach.

I said it, and they said, "Welcome to David et Jonathan."

After dinner, we moved to the other room where we could sit and talk more in depth. As we had before dinner, we started with a prayer, asking God to be with us and guide us as we searched for a way to reconcile our faith and our reality. And then we talked. Well, mostly they talked and I listened. I'm so new on this journey that I don't feel like I have a lot to share yet, but they do. They have these wonderful (and sometimes horrendous) stories to tell of acceptance and rejection.

I've decided I want to be like Alexandre when I grow up. He had started in the seminary, studying to be a priest, when he met his husband, a frequent visitor for retreats. After much reflection and discussion with his spiritual advisor, he realized his path to serving God wasn't as a priest but as one of the laity, helping people like him make the same journey. He and his husband, who wasn't at the meeting last night but apparently usually comes, founded the Grenoble chapter of David et Jonathan almost fifteen years ago. That's what I want. Not necessarily to found a chapter of David et Jonathan, but to have that kind of relationship and that kind of peace and surety.

Of course, that means I have to find someone who feels the same way about me, someone who can share my life the way Alexandre's husband shares his. I said something to that effect when it was my turn to share, explaining that I was just starting on this journey, but that what I wanted was to build a life with someone. Everyone nodded in agreement, but Alexandre reminded me there wasn't any rush, that I could afford to take my time and find the right person. A PACS, the French civil union that's open to gays as well as straights, can be dissolved like any marriage, but that isn't what we're called to enter into. Like all Christians, we're called to enter a covenant with our spouse, and those are not so easy to dissolve. Not that a PACS would be recognized in Texas, or probably anywhere else in the US, but that isn't the point. The point is that whatever name that relationship has from a legal standpoint, in my heart, it should be the same marriage covenant blessed by any minister in any church anywhere in the world.

It was reassuring to hear. I don't have to rush. I don't have to figure Pierre out right away, or even ever. If I can't, if he's more interested in playing games than in building a relationship, I don't have to grasp at straws, hoping he's the one. I can wait until the right one comes along.

I asked Alexandre after the evening was over what he knew about the Pole Étudiant Catholique and whether I'd be welcomed there. He assured me I would, although he said it had been several years since he'd been involved there because he wasn't exactly a student anymore. He mentioned the priest from l'église St Louis, the same one I met on Sunday, as the one in charge of the group. I was glad to hear I'd judged the situation with the priest correctly.

It's getting late. I should go to sleep. Work will come early tomorrow and it's nearly midnight now. I don't regret going, even if I'm tired tomorrow. I needed the affirmation I got tonight. I don't think I realized just how much I needed it until I got it.

Thursday, July 4

Happy Fourth of July!

Of course it's just another work day here. Their national celebration, Bastille Day, except nobody in France calls it that, isn't for another ten days. I'm looking forward to it. Jean-Mathias and I were talking about it at lunch today when I mentioned how odd it was to be here and not doing anything to celebrate the Fourth. From what he said, it'll be quite a party. They start around 5:30 with a military parade (not sure how interested I am in that, although I guess it could be fun to simply be out in the streets with everyone) and a reception at l'Hôtel de Ville. I think that's like city hall. Then at 10:30, the fireworks start, followed by a huge dance/ball in the Jardin de Ville. He said the same group of friends who play soccer on the weekends are getting together to watch the fireworks and then go to the dance and that I'd be welcome to go along if I want. I think it sounds like a lot of fun, so I'll probably go, although I told him I wanted to see what the Moreaus have planned first. Not that I'm under any obligation to do things with them, but I also don't want to turn down so many invitations that they don't invite me to things anymore.

Pierre was home for dinner tonight. He said he'd missed me last night. That set the butterflies dancing again. I told him where I was, and I'm pretty sure he recognized the name David et Jonathan. He didn't say outright, but I'm sure he knew what it is.

Mme Moreau called us for dinner before we could talk any more than that, which is probably just as well. I needed a few minutes to calm my nerves and get myself settled again.

After dinner, Pierre brought up the CDs he'd lent me and followed me upstairs so we could talk about music some more. And we did, for a few minutes, but before long, he asked me if I had plans for the weekend. I told him about playing soccer with Jean-Mathias and his friends on Sunday, but that's all I have planned. He suggested we catch a movie on Saturday night.

I think I have a date on Saturday. A real date.

Pierre didn't use that word, but it felt like he was asking me out. Like he wanted the two of us to do something special. We talked about movies after that, avoiding the subject of the implications of the evening. At least I avoided it and Pierre let me. Or maybe Pierre avoided it and I let him. Anyway, one of the local cinemas is doing a retrospective of Jean-Paul Rappeneau. I admit to being clueless about French cinema, but even I know that name. Cyrano de Bergerac, Horseman on the Roof, A Matter of Resistance. They're showing all eight of the films he directed as well as several of the ones he wrote over the course of the weekend. We're going to see Cyrano de Bergerac because who can resist, although if Horseman on the Roof hadn't been on Sunday afternoon, I might have suggested that one. Vincent Perez isn't bad, but Olivier Martinez… need I say more?

So yeah, I have a date on Saturday night. I'm not entirely sure what that means. I mean, obviously it means I have a date on Saturday night (assuming I'm reading him right), but I still don't know what Pierre is looking for from me. For that matter, I'm not entirely sure what I'm looking for from him. I'm in France for a year. A lot can happen in a year, but I have plans for next year, plans I'm not sure I'm willing to change, and I have no idea what it would take for Pierre to be able to come to the US for more than a visit.

Wow, I'm getting ahead of myself, aren't I? We haven't even had our first date, much less a kiss or any other kind of step toward a romantic relationship, and I'm already trying to figure out how to get him moved to the US.

Actually, I'm not. Not in any concrete sense. More in the sense of reminding myself that I shouldn't expect to find anything permanent here, this year. This year should be about me, about getting comfortable with who I am so that when I go home, I'll be self-assured enough to begin searching for my soul mate there. I can go out with Pierre, even have a relationship with him, without it having to be "the one." And when I go home next June, it will be with a smile on my face for all the wonderful times we spent together.

So now I have to wait until Saturday and see what happens next.

Maybe I'll see what films are playing tomorrow night and ask Jean-Mathias and some of the others at work if they want to go. If I stay home and brood, I'll be so nervous by Saturday night that I'll never make it.

Friday, July 5

Jean-Mathias already has plans for tonight, so it's sit in my room and brood. Pierre wasn't home for dinner, and Serge and Elodie disappeared soon after we finished to do something with friends of theirs. I didn't ask to tag along. That would be too pathetic even for me. I graduated from college in May and they're still in high school. Not that I'd have said no if they asked me along, but I didn't feel right inviting myself. It won't kill me to spend one evening alone in my room, even if it feels like it at the moment.

I suppose I could go out by myself. I could go back to L'Absolu or go to the movies or go shopping even, since I have to find something to wear for tomorrow night. I can wear jeans, but I want something nicer than a T-shirt without wearing one of my button-down shirts. I hate shopping. At least at home, I could throw myself on Teresa's mercy and make her go shopping with me. I know the stereotype about gay men having great fashion sense, but I'll tell you right now, that's one stereotype that doesn't apply to me. I can get out of the house looking presentable in the sense that my shirt is tucked in and my pants and shirt don't clash, but I don't know the slightest thing about the latest fashion.

The problem is I still don't know if tomorrow is a date or not. If it isn't, I'm going to feel pretty silly if I dress up, and if it is, I'd feel just as ridiculous dressed down. I seem to remember reading or hearing that French teens tend to go out in groups more than as couples, but at some point that has to change. And I saw definite couples among Pierre's friends at his birthday party. Camille, one of Pierre's friends, danced with anyone who asked, but she kissed Abdou, practically sitting on his lap any time she wasn't dancing. That seems awfully paired up to me.

So if, by this point in their lives, they do start to pair up, then tomorrow night could be a date. Pierre definitely danced with other guys at L'Absolu on Saturday far too provocatively to be straight. I guess he could be bisexual, but he's definitely interested in guys. And he did ask me if I wanted to go with him to see a movie. He didn't mention anyone else, not like when Jean-Mathias suggested playing soccer with "us." Of course, that could be Pierre. And even if it is just Pierre and me, that doesn't make it a date. I asked Jean-Mathias if he wanted to see a movie with me tonight without that being a date, even if it would have been just the two of us.

I guess I wait and see, except I'm not even sure how I'll know once it arrives. I mean, if he kisses me or holds my hand, that would obviously make it a date, but if he doesn't, does that mean it isn't a date?

I have a feeling I should have figured this all out years ago, but I'm not sure I would have even if I'd grown up in a different environment. Even for the kids with much less conservative parents, being gay wasn't something they talked about, at least not openly. I guess if I'd gone to a different college, I might have figured some of this out then, but I didn't, and I don't regret it. Not really. I'd have been just as clueless four years ago as I am now, without the maturity I gained in college to help me deal with it.

This will work out, one way or another. I came here to do exactly what I'm doing: figure out how to live my life as a gay man. If tomorrow night is a false start, that's fine. There are plenty of those in life. I'll just start again.

Saturday, July 6

I found this store called, of all things, Somewhere. Not Quelque part, but Somewhere. In English. One of the salespeople took pity on me and helped me find something for tonight. The good news is that everything was en solde. In France (as crazy as this sounds) they have two huge sales a year, one in the winter and one in the summer, with huge discounts for five weeks, in every store in the country. So it's the beginning of the summer sales, with fifty and sixty percent discounts on everything in the store. With Dr. Besson's assurances that my salary would arrive on time at the end of July, I took advantage of the salesman's expertise and bought quite a few new shirts and a couple pairs of pants, somewhere between jeans and dress trousers, and a new lightweight jacket—not a sports coat, but something I can wear in the evenings when it's cool or in the fall. That was way more money than I'd planned on spending when I left the house this morning, but it's stuff I need and will use. So now I have to decide what to wear tonight. The salesman suggested the new khaki trousers and plum-colored polo. I've never owned anything plum in my life, but I tried it on, and he convinced me it was really flattering. I do kind of like the way it looks with my fair skin, although I'm not a great judge of stuff like that. I'll have to trust that the man knew what he was talking about.

And if he was wrong, I'll be embarrassed tonight.

I could go with a more conservative shirt. I got several different colors and styles of polos. Except that I like the way the plum looks.

I'm turning into such a girl. I don't think I like this side of myself. I think it's time to go for a swim. I found the nearest pool and I have my swim trunks. I'll feel better for some exercise.

I had a good swim. I went ahead and got a membership to the pool. Yes, I know, I'm supposed to be saving my money, but I could get a membership that would end up costing me less than 5 euros a week or I could pay 2 euros every time I go to swim. As close as the pool is, I'll swim at least three times a week, especially once it starts to get cold, so that will save me money in the long run. I'm back at the house, showered and dressed (in my plum shirt) and ready to go. Now I just have to wait for Pierre to get here. I think next time I'll suggest we meet wherever we're going, if only so I don't end up feeling like I'm waiting to be picked up. Teresa would beat me for saying that makes me feel like the girl, particularly since I know of more than one occasion when she picked up her date because she had a car and he didn't, but that seems to be beside the point at the moment. I don't like feeling passive, and sitting here waiting for Pierre to arrive instead of going somewhere to meet him makes me feel that way. Even if I ended up early or he was late, and I had to wait for him wherever we were meeting, it wouldn't be the same as waiting at home. At least I don't think it would be the same. It never felt this… fraught when I waited for friends wherever we were supposed to be meeting.

Or is that because this is a date (I hope) and I'd feel the same way if I was waiting for Pierre at the movie theater?

When did I get to be so emo? If this is part of being an adult, maybe I should go back to college.

Actually, I suspect I'd feel this way even if I was straight, only I'd be trying to figure out if a girl liked me instead of if a guy did. And maybe I'd have figured it out a little sooner, since dating wasn't prohibited on campus. Just having sex with someone other than your spouse. Unfortunately for me, they'd never acknowledge any kind of homosexual conduct as appropriate because it would never lead to marriage, which they defined very clearly in the Honor Code as one man and one woman. I accepted that as a freshman because I hadn't ever allowed myself to think beyond the box I'd always been taught was true. By the time I was a junior, I questioned it, but I wasn't to the point of changing schools because of it. And now, here, I've met people who reject that one aspect of the Honor Code without rejecting all the spirituality and tradition behind it.

I was going somewhere with that train of thought, but I sure don't know where it was now, except to say that I'm ready for it to be time to go because I'm nervous (well, duh, read this entry) and waiting only makes it worse.

Oops, Pierre's here. Later!

I'm grinning from ear to ear. I know it's late and I have to get up for church tomorrow morning, but if I oversleep, I can always go to the evening Mass.

I have had my first date as a gay man.

The movie was fabulous, of course. I knew that even before I went tonight, but this is the first time I've ever seen it without subtitles. I couldn't follow everything they said, but then again, I spent more than a little time distracted by Pierre's arm around my shoulder.

So yeah, it was a date.

From what I wrote earlier, he met me at the house. We took the bus again because of parking. The retrospective was in the downtown area, which is pedestrian only, so even if we drove, we'd have ended up walking to the theater. This way we didn't have to worry about parking. We got downtown early, so we went by one of the nearby cafés to have a drink. Pierre introduced me to something called a kir. He promised it wouldn't give me a headache because it's wine based. He was right. So anyway, we each had a kir and then went to the movie. Pierre insisted on treating me to both, which was my first hint it was a date. Or maybe I should say my first hint tonight since I'd already had a few hints before.

About the time Cyrano took Christian's place underneath Roxane's balcony, Pierre put his arm around my shoulders.

I melted right along with her, and not because of the beautiful words spoken on screen, even if I think it's some of the most beautiful love poetry ever written. What is it about sitting in a dark movie theater with a guy's arm around your shoulders? It doesn't seem like it should be all that special, but it was. I felt like the luckiest guy in the room, even if no one else realized it. I had this really cute (really cute!) guy interested in me. I refuse to write "boring old me," even if it feels that way sometimes. I'm obviously not "boring old me," because Pierre wanted to take me out.

He had his hair down tonight. Did I mention that he has shoulder length curly hair? After four years of school rules saying no male's hair could touch the collar of his shirt, Pierre's hair just makes me want to bury my fingers in it. Some days, he pulls it back into this messy ponytail, with wisps falling out to curl around his face. Other days, like today, he doesn't pull it back at all, and it frames his face perfectly. I'm not an artist, but I learned enough in my art history class to appreciate composition when I see it, and the combination of his hair and eyes is the right composition for me, that's for sure.

I guess that makes it official. I'm in the middle of my first real crush.

So we watched the second half of the movie with Pierre's arm around my shoulder, and he didn't even laugh at me when I cried at Cyrano's death. Not that it was a laughing matter even if I hadn't cried, because I'll repeat what I said before. Some of the most beautiful poetry in the world.

> J'ignorais la douceur feminine. Ma mère
> Ne m'a pas trouvé beau; je n'ai pas eu de sœur
> Plus tard, j'ai redouté l'amante à l'œil moqueur.
> Je vous dois d'avoir eu tout au moins une amie.
> Grâce à vous, une robe a passé dans ma vie.

I'm a geek. Sue me. I'm teary-eyed just writing down the lines from the film. (Okay, I cheated and looked them up, but I'm still teary-eyed.) And then when Roxane asks him why he didn't say anything after Christian died since the tears in the ink were his, Cyrano reminded her that the blood was Christian's. Yes, it's a tragedy, and there's a part of me that recognizes the hubris and that Cyrano's unhappiness really was his own fault, but it's such a beautiful story, and Rappeneau did such an amazing job converting the play to film.

Wow, am I rambling! I've completely lost track of my description of the evening, except that the movie was a huge part of that, not just in terms of the time we spent watching it but in terms of the mood of the evening.

We didn't go see some slapstick comedy or an action thriller or a political satire. We went to see one of the great French romances, and honestly, from a purely literary perspective, it's a story that outclasses Romeo and Juliet any day of the week. So that set a contemplative, emotional tone to the evening. When we left the theater, it was to walk quietly through the pedestrian section of town, not really talking, just being together. We held hands in the dark as we walked. When we got to the edge of the pedestrian zone, we just kept walking. It's not all that far from home, but we didn't go straight home. Instead we wandered along the Isère. With the sun having set behind the mountains but the sky still barely light and the lights from all the cafés and streetlamps reflecting in the water, I'm not sure it could have been any more romantic.

The breeze off the mountains was cool enough to raise goose bumps on my arm. Pierre noticed and teased me a little, asking how I was going to survive the snow in winter, but he also put his arm around me again to share his body heat as we walked. And we talked. We talked about the movie and about French literature. (He has me almost convinced to give Alexandre Dumas another try. The text was too dense when I first tried to read it, but I know more French now than I did then.) And then we talked about Foot 38, the soccer, er, I guess I should say football, team in Grenoble. Pierre is a huge fan, especially of their team captain, Nicolas Dieuze. I teased him back about having a thing for Dieuze. I can't be sure since it was dark, but I think he blushed.

I really don't know how long we walked because I didn't look to see what time it was when we left the movie theater, but it was nearly midnight by the time we got back to the Moreaus' house. I wondered if Pierre would come in or try to kiss me goodnight, but he didn't do either, squeezing my hand instead and promising he'd see me for Sunday lunch the next day.

A part of me is disappointed. How can I not be? A kiss would have been a perfect ending to a perfect evening, but most of me appreciates his restraint. You only get one first kiss. I'll know when I'm ready for mine, and while I might be ready soon, I wasn't tonight. Not really.

And on that note, I should put this away and go to sleep. It's after one and if I'm going to have Sunday dinner with the Moreaus and play soc-football with Jean-Mathias, I should really go to church in the morning, which means getting up around nine. Yeah, definitely time for bed.

And hopefully sweet dreams.

Sunday, July 7

Another day come and gone, and I'm as confused now as I was elated last night. Pierre came to Sunday lunch today and acted like last night never happened. I mean, not completely. He talked about the movie we went to see (and the fact that we went to see it together), but he didn't allude to it being a date or anything other than a movie at all. I realize he was talking to his parents and siblings, but even so, a smile or something to let me know he remembered the rest would have been nice. As it is, I have no idea if last night meant anything to him at all, or if.... I don't even know "or if" what. I mean, he put his arm around my shoulders and held my hand and gave every indication of being really into me last night, and then today, nothing. I might get that if it had been a one-night stand or something, but he didn't even kiss me, and not because I refused. I doubt I would have last night, although if he came up here now, I'd be a lot more hesitant about it. So it wasn't a "love 'em and leave 'em" thing. The problem is I still don't know what it was.

It's so much easier being friends with Jean-Mathias. We had another great pickup match today at the football field. A lot of the players were repeats from last week (and they remembered me and welcomed me back), but there were also some new faces, to me anyway. People who weren't available last Sunday, maybe, because while they weren't there last week, it was pretty obvious from everyone else's reactions that they're there often.

So anyway, I'm lost again where the whole relationship thing is concerned. I thought it meant something to Pierre, but I was obviously wrong, so now I have to decide what to do next. The way I see it, I have a couple of choices. I can forget about it entirely and move on to whatever's next. I can wait to see if he asks me out again (although I have no idea how long would be a reasonable amount of time to wait). Or I can ask him out.

That's a nerve-wracking thought. I don't even know what I'd ask him to do. I hardly have any idea what's going on around town or where the good places to go are. I could ask Serge and Elodie, maybe, except that the places a high school student would choose aren't necessarily the places I'd want to go. Maybe Jean-Mathias could give me some suggestions. Someplace adult.

I don't mean adult like X-rated, but adult like not aimed at teenagers. A classy restaurant or a wine tasting or a… I don't know, but something we could do together as a date.

I'll think about asking him tomorrow at lunch.

Monday, July 8

I came out to Jean-Mathias today. I mean, I didn't flat out tell him I was gay, but I asked him for suggestions on somewhere to go on a date, and he replied with "Who's the lucky girl?" So I told him it wasn't a girl. He blinked a couple of times, like he was surprised, then grinned and asked me who the lucky guy was. So I told him. All of it, from the birthday party to the date to Pierre's confusing reaction after.

Jean-Mathias suggested Pierre might be trying not to crowd me or make me feel pressured. I hadn't considered that, since I wasn't feeling that way at all. It makes me feel a little better anyway. So then he suggested a theater festival that's going on next weekend. I love it that Grenoble has so much going on, in the summer anyway. It's exciting and so different from home.

So now all I have to do is wait for Pierre to come to dinner again so I can ask if he'd like to go to one of the presentations next weekend. Jean-Mathias also gave me the names of a couple of nice restaurants where we could eat before or after the play.

You know the best part of it, though? He didn't care. I told him about Pierre and he barely blinked an eye. I keep telling myself I'll run into people who aren't accepting of my orientation, but it hasn't happened yet. Well, not since I made the decision to come out. I knew plenty of people in high school and college who were homophobic.

I'm a little nervous about Wednesday night, despite the reassurances of Alexandre and everyone at David et Jonathan. It's one thing to be accepted by a niche group. It's another thing to be accepted by a mainstream religious group. I don't have to tell them right away. I don't have to tell them at all if I'm not comfortable. And I don't have to go back if I'm not welcome there as I am. This isn't college. Nobody's going to fine me for missing chapel. I just have to keep reminding myself of that.

Wednesday, July 10

Pierre didn't come to dinner yesterday and tonight I had dinner with the Pole Étudiant group. It was different than David et Jonathan. A lot more people, for one thing, and all college age instead of from different stages of life, but I'm not so far removed from that situation that I can't fit in. Besides, some of them are in longer degree programs and so are my age or older simply because they can't finish medical school or law school in four years. The theme tonight was how God acts in our lives. It was very interesting and affirming to listen to the different stories. I remember hearing a preacher when I was in middle school who said there were as many different ways to God as there were people on the path. The stories tonight prove that all over again.

Mostly I listened tonight. I wasn't quite ready to come out to a group of people I didn't know with no idea how they'd react, but I will definitely go back next week, and maybe in a few weeks I'll be ready.

Thursday, July 11

Pierre came home for dinner tonight, and I managed to talk to him for a few minutes without everyone else around. I mentioned the festival this weekend. It turns out he has plans for the entire weekend. He's going to Antibes with Caroline, Genevieve, and Abdul, three of his friends I met at his birthday party. I guess he's had the plans for a while, although he didn't say that exactly, but either way, I don't have a date for the weekend after all.

I could live with that. I mean, I can hardly claim all his time when he didn't even know me before two weeks ago, but it's still a little disconcerting that he didn't suggest something else, maybe next weekend, when he told me he couldn't go out with me this weekend.

If this continues, I'm going to turn to cursing. I just wish I knew what was going on in his head. I don't mind spending the weekend without him. I'll probably end up spending it with Jean-Mathias, at least the football game on Sunday, but I'd like to know if I'm wasting my time, because if I am, I'll gladly look somewhere else for a relationship. There's plenty going on in the gay community here too, with Cigale and its member associations. I could get involved there, maybe meet someone, if Pierre isn't interested in me. I could go back to L'Absolu or one of the other clubs I found on the GLBT web site.

I suppose there's nothing to stop me from doing those things regardless of Pierre's interest. After all, I'm not even sure we're dating. We certainly haven't made any promises. And even if we had, a lot of the stuff Cigale does is more along the lines of social activism. Despite the positive reactions I've had here so far, I know social activism is as important here as it is at home.

Maybe I'll see what Cigale has going on Saturday.

Friday, July 12

I'm going camping this weekend.

Jean-Mathias asked me at lunch today if I'd seen Pierre and what his reaction was to my suggestion, so I told him about Pierre going out of town and how I wasn't quite sure how to take that. He asked me if I had any plans now that I wasn't going out with Pierre. Obviously I didn't, so he suggested I join him and a couple of other guys for some hiking and camping this weekend.

I don't have any gear, but he told me not to worry about that. One of his friends' family has a sort of cabin up in the mountains. The only way to get to it is to hike in or ride in on horseback. No electricity, well water, pretty much the definition of rural, but he assured me there are enough beds for one more and clean sheets for the beds, so as long as I'm willing to chip in for food and help carry the gear, I'm welcome. We're leaving at six in the morning, so I'm going to bed early.

I'm almost glad Pierre wasn't free this weekend after all because this sounds like it's going to be great fun. I'll bring my journal, but depending on space, I may decide not to carry it up the mountain. If so, I'll write in detail on Sunday when we get home. Jean-Mathias said we wouldn't stay late since Sunday night is the July 14 party. With it being on a Sunday this year, we get Monday off work, so that's good. A day to recover from staying up and dancing in the streets until who knows what time of night.

Saturday, July 13

There was space in my pack for my journal (not like it's large). Jean-Mathias picked me up this morning at six as planned, and then we picked up Xavier and Romain, Jean-Mathias's friends. The gîte belongs to Romain's family. We drove for about an hour up into the mountains toward Courchevel, although we didn't go quite that far. Romain's family makes this trip often enough that they have an agreement with a man in some little town to leave their car in the bakery parking lot when they go up into the mountains. By eight, we'd started the hike. It took almost three hours to get up here, but it was worth every step. We're so high up in the mountains I swear I can touch the clouds. And the view is spectacular. The Alps spread out all around us, below us mostly. Mont Blanc is visible in the distance, but most of the closer mountains are lower than we are. We got unloaded and set up for the weekend, made the beds we'll use, that sort of thing. Romain and Xavier are kicking around a ball. I don't know where Jean-Mathias disappeared to, and I'm sitting here in the sun, soaking up the rays for all I'm worth. I'm not vain. I don't care about a tan or anything like that. It just feels good to sit in the sun and relax. It's been a busy few weeks and it's peaceful here.

I don't think I realized how much I needed that right now. Nothing to do, no one to care about how well I speak French (or don't speak it as the case may be), no boyfriend (or not boyfriend) to worry about. Nothing but the sun, the sound of Xavier and Romain ribbing each other over how badly they play football, and the birds chirping. There isn't even the wind in the trees because we passed the tree line.

The gîte is bare bones, like Jean-Mathias said. It's a single level with three rooms—a kitchen and two bedrooms. It's made of yellow stone and is practically tucked into the mountain. I haven't poked around in the bedrooms yet (I was on kitchen duty), but I wouldn't be surprised if the back walls are actually the rock face of the mountain. The roof abuts the side of the mountain. Rustic is probably a good word for it, but I like it. I wouldn't want to live here year round, obviously, with no running water and no electricity, but I could see coming up here on weekends during the summer months to relax. The hike was energizing despite the steep ascent, and the air smells so fresh.

I didn't really think about it in Grenoble, but up here, away from all the city smells, I can tell the difference. It's clean up here. Pure.

And there's Jean-Mathias. He just challenged Romain and Xavier to a football match, them against him and me. I think he just set me up to make a fool of myself, but I'll give it my best shot.

Man, what a day!

All the fresh air has exhausted me. Either that or the hours of playing football this afternoon. We made dinner on this old camp stove that someone must have lugged up here once upon a time. We brought fresh propane, but the pots and the stove were already here. By the time we were done cooking, the sun had started to set, so Romain pulled out this old oil lantern. I'm sitting here in the deepening dusk, writing in my journal by the light of an old-fashioned lamp. This is too cool.

And the best part? Jean-Mathias isn't at all weirded out by the fact that I'm gay and we're all camping together. No odd looks. No reminders that he's straight. Nothing to make me feel uncomfortable about who I am. I mean, not that I'd do anything without his consent regardless of his orientation, but I can imagine it could make a straight guy uncomfortable to share a bedroom with a gay guy.

I don't know if he told Xavier and Romain about me, but if he did, it doesn't matter to them, and if he didn't, they don't need to know. They're great guys and I've had a blast with them today, but I'm not attracted to them so it's a moot point.

Now if Pierre was up here—

Damn it. I told myself I wasn't going to think about him this weekend. He's spending a weekend with his friends and I'm spending a weekend with mine, and that's perfectly fine. Even married couples don't spend every minute of every day together. Dad has gone to continuing education workshops without Mom and vice versa. Dad goes off on his trainspotting weekends, and Mom goes antiquing with her college roommates.

So why does it bother me so much that he's off with someone else?

Because he didn't tell me about it until I tried to make plans for us this weekend. Because he didn't seem to care enough about us to make future plans. Because it felt like he blew me off in the way he told me about it when I asked him out for this weekend.

Okay, this is getting me nowhere and everyone else is heading to bed. I'm stopping now to do the same. I'll worry about Pierre later.

Sunday, July 14

Happy National Holiday!

That's what they say in France. Bonne fête nationale! We've had breakfast and are hanging out for probably another hour before we head back down the mountain. No running water means no shower this morning, and everyone wants a chance to clean up before the party starts tonight. Granted, that's not until 10:30 for the fireworks and dancing, but Romain apparently always attends the parade, so he has to be ready to go at 5 and it will take us several hours to hike back, plus we have to drive back into town.

I don't care that it's a short weekend. It's been fun, definitely something I'd do again if I'm invited.

I have decided self-pity does not become me. If Pierre doesn't want to do things with me, that's his business. My business is how I react to that. My self-worth doesn't—and shouldn't—depend on anyone else but me. So I'll go home, take a shower, meet Jean-Mathias and his friends for the party tonight. Tomorrow I'll enjoy my day off, and Tuesday I'll go back to work like usual. If Pierre decides to show up and asks me out again, I'll think about it, but the ball's in his court. I showed him I was interested by asking him out for this weekend. So, enough of this. I'm going to play football with Romain since Xavier is being lazy this morning.

Monday, July 15

The party last night was a blast! Sort of like the party in Paris for Pride except with French flags instead of rainbow flags. And with fireworks.

I met up with Jean-Mathias, Xavier, Romain, and some of the others from football and we watched the fireworks before going on to the Jardin de Ville where the dancing took place. I think the fireworks actually happened in the garden too, but it's always easier to see fireworks from a distance.

There weren't as many same-sex couples last night as there were at Pride in Paris, but there were some, and nobody seemed to care. And of course, this wasn't a GLBT event, so it would make sense that we'd be in the minority. I don't know exact demographics, but I can't imagine homosexual couples make up more than a fraction of the population here. So I danced with some of the girls and generally had a great time. I'm definitely glad I went.

Today is a lazy day. Nothing to do but rest and enjoy the sunshine. I'm sitting in the Moreaus' garden in a pair of cutoffs and nothing else. The sun is warm, but not oppressively so, and life is good.

Thursday, July 18

Pierre was home for dinner again tonight, the first time this week. He seems to like Thursdays. Anyway, he asked if I'd had a good weekend, so I told him about going camping with Jean-Mathias, Xavier, and Romain. That seemed to shake him up a little, so he asked what I was doing next weekend. I don't have plans other than maybe playing soccer with Jean-Mathias, so he asked if I want to spend the weekend at his uncle's vineyard with him.

I admit it. I almost said no just because he turned me down for last weekend, but I didn't because, let's face it, a weekend at a vineyard sounds amazing.

Pierre's uncle seemed nice at the party, and he said he wouldn't mind showing me around and explaining things to me, so even if this doesn't turn out to be a date like I think it will be, I'll still learn something and hopefully have a good time. And if it is a date, it should be a really nice one.

I guess I ought to make it clear that I won't sleep with him. I mean, two beds in the same room like with Jean-Mathias at the gîte would be fine, but I'm not ready for the intimacy of sleeping in the same bed with him, even if all we do is sleep.

Work is going well. Nothing special to really write about which is why I skipped Tuesday. Yesterday was a good day, with the Pole Étudiant in the evening, but by the time I got home, it was really too late to write anything. We had another interesting, thought-provoking discussion. I'm glad I decided to join. I need that kind of spiritual companionship.

It's late, once again, so I'm going to head to bed. I'll try to do better with my journal.

Thursday, July 25

Wow, a whole week this time without writing. I'm getting worse rather than better, but things have been crazy at work. It turns out most people take four weeks of vacation for the month of August, and so everyone is trying to wrap up their projects and teach me and one other tech how to do what can't be wrapped up in their absence. Technically we aren't supposed to work overtime, French labor laws and all that, but I've worked plenty this week! Dr. Besson said we'd balance it out in August with shorter hours since there would be less work to do. I'm not sure how taking on the responsibilities of everyone who won't be around counts as less work, but I'll figure that out next week.

Jean-Mathias is actually only taking one week of vacation now because he's saving the rest for his sister's wedding in Africa at Christmas. She works in Bénin with Médecins sans Frontières and fell in love with a man there. I think that's really exciting. She went for what was supposed to be a two-year stay, and now she's making it her home. Jean-Mathias said she fell in love with the people and the country and started talking about extending her stay even before she met Imamu, but that meeting him clenched the deal for her. I know I'm a hopeless romantic, but it's such a beautiful story. So that means I'll at least have him around to help me for most of the month. He's only leaving the second to last week of August.

I spoke with Mme Moreau today, and they are going to the beach in Bretagne for the month, but she assured me it was fine for me to stay in the house, to use the kitchen and everything. I'll have to buy my own groceries, but since breakfast and dinner are included in my rent, she said she wouldn't charge me as much for the month since I'd be buying my own food. That was generous of her. She certainly didn't have to help me out that way, although since I got my first allocation familiale check today (the one that helps subsidize my rent), I'm actually in slightly better shape financially than I expected to be at this point.

I didn't ask her if Pierre was going with the rest of the family. I'm a little afraid to ask, but more than that, I want him to tell me himself. It's not that I don't want him to go. I mean, this is a family tradition and he didn't know me until a month ago, but I would like him to do me the courtesy of telling me he'll be gone for part or all of the month.

Jean-Mathias told me his plans, and we're just friends. Then again, all the craziness at work probably prompted that conversation, because I don't know what Xavier's or Romain's plans are. It hasn't come up at the football games on Sunday.

I really need to stop obsessing about this and pack for the trip to the vineyard. Pierre said he'd be here tomorrow at six to pick me up, so I won't have time to do anything except throw in my toiletries that I use in the morning.

I have no idea what I should take with me. I mean, it's July so it's pretty warm outside, and if the idea is to see how the vineyard works, I imagine we'll be outside quite a bit, so shorts and T-shirts would seem logical. But I'm going at Pierre's invitation, so it's also sort of a date, and I wouldn't wear shorts and a T-shirt on a date. I guess I could take some nicer things as well and then dress according to how everyone else is attired. That way I'd have a choice. My duffel is big enough to put in extra.

I'll do that.

All packed. Well, except for my toothbrush and shampoo. I'll toss those in after I shower in the morning. Now I just have to sleep tonight. I'd hoped going for a swim after work today would tire me out enough that I wouldn't toss and turn nervously, but I can already tell that isn't going to work. My stomach is all tied in knots. I'm going away for the weekend with a guy who might be (or become) my boyfriend. This is nothing like going away two weekends ago with Jean-Mathias. Not in my head, anyway. I wasn't nervous at all then, and now I'm all but wringing my hands. Not a terribly masculine reaction, but I can't pace and write at the same time, so I'll settle for tapping my fingers nervously on the desk.

I should try to sleep except I know I'll just lie in bed and stare at the ceiling if I do. If I don't, though, I'll end up sitting here babbling all night.

Bedtime it is.

Friday, July 26

We drove to the vineyard tonight. It's outside of Crozes-Hermitage, which I understand is a well-known wine-producing area. It took a little over an hour, but we talked the whole way so the time flew by.

Pierre did tell me, without prompting, that he would be with his parents in Bretagne for part of next month. The first part, unfortunately, from my perspective, but at least he'll be back when Jean-Mathias is gone so I'll have someone to spend time with.

We got to Hugues's house in time for dinner. He and his wife, Virginie, both insisted I call them by their first names. Not sure I'm entirely comfortable with that, but I won't insult their hospitality by refusing. It helps that Pierre calls them that too, without any honorific attached. No Tati or Tonton, which is what I learned French children use with their aunts and uncles. Not that Pierre is a child anymore, but they are still his aunt and uncle.

Anyway, we had a lovely, simple dinner, with plenty of wine. Knowing my ignorance, Hugues explained the differences in the wines we had and how the years and the mineral content in the soil and other factors could change the flavors of different wines. One of the wines wasn't from his property, which surprised me a little, although after listening to the conversation about pairing wine and food and having the right combination of tannins and sugars and body to go with different dishes, I can see how one wine producer couldn't make all the different varieties of wines. And the soup we had as a first course was very light. The heavier red wine from his vineyard definitely wouldn't have gone well with it.

Wow. I have learned something today. Cool. I wonder what else I'll learn this weekend.

I didn't even have to mention preferring my own room. Virginie had a room made up for me, a beautiful, open room with a balcony that looks out over the courtyard of the house. Not something I'd expect to see at home, but I'm getting used to the idea that this is the way houses, at least older, country houses, are built here. The house and garden walls create a graveled courtyard where they leave the cars. Then the garden is on the other side of the house. With this being a vineyard, there are lots of other buildings as well, used to store the wine casks and to process the wine. Hugues promised me a tour of all of those tomorrow.

I'm still a little nervous to see what the rest of the weekend will bring, but Hugues and Virginie couldn't have been more welcoming, so even if all I do is learn a lot about wine, it will be a good weekend.

Saturday, July 27

What a day! I came inside after spending all day out in the fields and barns with Hugues and Pierre, learning all about how he cultivates the grapes and then makes wine. I've got a bit of time before dinner, though I need to shower still, because there's no way I'm showing up at the dinner table all sweaty and caked in mud.

I have a much greater appreciation for the work that goes into winemaking now, and after listening to everything Hugues had to say and tasting some of the different wines he produces, I'm beginning to get a sense of the lingo. It'll take more than one wine tasting before I'm conversant, but at least I don't feel completely ignorant anymore.

I should jump in the shower. Dinner's in half an hour, and I don't want to be late. I'll finish this up later.

I'm not sure how to start. All the stuff I was going to write about? So not important now. Pierre kissed me.

After dinner, he suggested we go for a walk. We wandered out into the garden and then through the garden gate into the fields. The sun was setting over the river, which you can barely see from the top of the hills in the vineyard, and there was a breeze off the mountains, breaking the heat. As soon as we were out of the garden, Pierre reached for my hand, his fingers threading through mine and his thumb stroking the base of my thumb. Talk about sparks shooting all along my arm.

We walked mostly in silence, enjoying the quiet and the beauty of the evening (at least I was. I'm assuming he felt the same way.) We got to one of the rock walls that delineates the different appellations of wine in the area, and Pierre leaned against it, urging me to do the same. We stood there for I don't know how long, his thumb still stroking, mine doing a little encouraging in return, when he turned to face me, cradled my cheek with one hand, and kissed me.

I don't think my heart has ever pounded so hard in my life. He pulled away to look at me, like he wanted to make sure I wanted him to kiss me, so I imitated his position and kissed him back.

He'd taken a shower before dinner, but he hadn't shaved, so his cheek was stubbly beneath my hand, like I needed that reminder to know I was kissing a man. Not that I have any real idea what it would feel like to kiss a woman, but it certainly wouldn't involve a five o'clock shadow.

I don't really know how long we stood there, exchanging soft kisses, arms around each other's waists, but it eventually started to get dark enough that heading back inside was necessary. We were out among the vines, after all, not in the garden where there was light from the house.

Pierre put his arm around my waist as we walked back, so I reciprocated because it felt too good not to. Every so often, he'd stop and kiss me again, or I'd stop and kiss him. By the time we came back, it was pitch black. Fortunately Pierre knew where we were going because with only the moonlight to help us, I never would have found my way.

He kissed me one final time at the door to my room, telling me to sleep well and he'd see me in the morning.

My first kiss.

I'm grinning ear to ear and haven't stopped since the door shut behind Pierre. I keep losing the thread of this entry to stare off into space with, I'm quite sure, a goofy grin on my face.

In college, I didn't really let myself dream of what it would be like because I knew it wouldn't happen then. Couldn't happen then, and I was okay with that because I wasn't ready to come out. I needed that time to mature and come to terms with who I really am. If I'd gone somewhere else to school and had messed around like a lot of my friends did, I know I'd have ended up regretting some of those times. I don't know what will happen next week or next month or six months from now. I don't know if this relationship with Pierre will do for me what meeting Imamu did for Nicole, Jean-Mathias's sister, and that's fine if it doesn't, but at least I know it could.

I'm not sure that makes any sense to anyone but me. I'm not in love with Pierre because I don't know him well enough yet to say that, but I know I <u>could</u> fall in love with him. I'm already falling in love with France. So there's the possibility that this could be "the one." In college, I couldn't have said that, so I'm glad I didn't get or give my first kiss in some club somewhere in a situation that wouldn't have led to anything. Maybe Pierre and I will work out, maybe we won't. But we might.

I doubt I'll sleep any better tonight than I did on Thursday, out of excitement now rather than nerves. I keep reliving the feeling of Pierre's lips on mine. Not exactly conducive to restful sleep. It's a little difficult to sleep with a hard-on, and since I can't stop thinking about him, it's not going away. I'm not in my own bed (or somewhere impersonal like a hotel), so I don't exactly feel comfortable messing up the sheets, and the bathroom isn't en suite, so I don't know that I'd have enough privacy in the shower.

I guess I need to think about something else for a while.

Yeah, right. Like that's going to happen tonight.

I guess I'll go toss and turn until exhaustion takes over.

Sunday, July 28

We're back at home now. Pierre dropped me off half an hour ago. Of course M. and Mme Moreau wanted to know how the weekend had gone and if I enjoyed the vineyard and what I'd learned, so I had to sit and talk with them for a few minutes, even though all I wanted to do was come up here and bask in my memories of the weekend.

Despite my predictions last night, I actually fell asleep pretty quickly and slept surprisingly well. I guess the end of my uncertainty finally let the exhaustion kick in.

We slept in this morning, eating more of a brunch than breakfast, before spending the day lazing around the garden with Hugues and Virginie. Their kids joined us eventually—they're all a little older than Pierre—and started a round of croquet. I can't remember when I last laughed so hard.

Pierre is definitely the class clown, or would be if we were in class. He had us all in stitches, cracking jokes and being silly as we played. It's a side of him I hadn't seen before, and I really enjoyed it. I know I come off as all serious and stuff, but I like to have fun as much as the next guy, and I wouldn't want to be with someone who couldn't relax and let his hair down.

So to speak.

Because when Pierre lets his hair down literally, it's all I can do not to go run my fingers through it. I've developed a real hair fetish apparently. Not that this is a bad thing. It's just an unexpected thing. I've never really been around men with long hair, but it never did anything for me in movies or on TV. Pierre's hair, on the other hand, does all kinds of things to me. I haven't gotten up the nerve to run my fingers through it yet, but I hope I'll have that chance soon.

Hugues and Virginie insisted on feeding us dinner before we left to come home. I have to admit, I was a little worried about Pierre drinking and then driving us home, but he only had one glass of wine, and a small one at that. I shouldn't be so uptight, but I lost a friend in high school to a drunk driver. It's not something you get over.

Fortunately it didn't have to come up tonight. It's not that I don't want to tell Pierre about Timmy, but telling him about Timmy as I questioned his ability to drive us home safely didn't seem like a good idea.

We'd driven maybe halfway home when Pierre pulled over at this scenic overlook. We got out and sat on the rock wall and watched the lightning flash over the mountains. Overhead, the sky was clear still, but we could see the storm in the distance. It was stunning. Almost as stunning as the realization that I was sitting there with Pierre's arm around my shoulders and mine around his waist. Every so often, he'd lean over and kiss me lightly, his fingers playing with the collar of my shirt. That doesn't seem like it should be any big deal, but it was. Oh was it ever! When we finally got up to head the rest of the way home, because the storm was getting closer and it was getting darker, I was so hard it hurt. I hope Pierre didn't notice. He didn't say anything if he did.

I've got to get myself under control. I don't want a relationship based purely on sex or sexual attraction. I wasn't raised that way. That isn't to say I don't want sex in my relationship. Of course I do. I'm a perfectly healthy man with all the typical drives, but I want it to mean something. I want it to be real when it happens. At least Pierre doesn't seem inclined to rush things or push me into more than I'm willing to give at the moment. I'll just have to hope it stays that way.

Now I have to figure out what I'm going to say when Jean-Mathias asks me how my weekend was. I mean, I can tell him about the vineyard and everything I learned easily enough, but he knows about Pierre and our first date, and he knows this was the second one. Do I tell him Pierre kissed me? He knows I'm gay, so he's got to realize that's part of it, but that doesn't mean he wants to hear details. How much can I tell him, a straight guy? And how much is it okay to tell anyone, even someone who wouldn't be disturbed by the details? It was a very personal, private moment. I'm not sure I'm ready to shout it from the housetops, not out of any sense of shame, but because it was so special, so private.

I guess if he asks, I'll just say things are good and leave it at that. If it reaches the point that I need someone to confide all the details in, maybe someone at David et Jonathan would be willing to listen, someone who's gay and been through this and can help me figure out the balance I want in my life.

Thursday, August 1

I came home to an empty house tonight. Even knowing I would, it's strange being here without the family. In just a month, I've gotten used to them being around, M. and Mme Moreau and Serge and Elodie anyway. Pierre was never around predictably to begin with. Not that I would complain about seeing him when he is here, but it's not quite the same with him being gone as with the others.

The lab was pretty much empty today too, everyone trying to get out of town before the weekend rush. Like I told Jean-Mathias, I think it would be worth it to wait until Monday just to miss the rush of everyone trying to miss the rush. He laughed and said the traffic jams were as much a part of the month of vacation as the beach. That may be one of those cultural things that simply defies translation because I can't imagine how sitting in traffic for six or eight hours instead of the usual three hour drive to the beach (if you're going to the Mediterranean, of course) could possibly be considered a good start to your vacation. It's probably different for the Moreaus since they're headed north toward Bretagne instead of south to the Côte d'Azur. Traffic might not be as bad going in that direction, at least not until they get past Paris.

Dr. Besson was as good as his word on work hours. He left a schedule to make up for the crazy hours we worked the last two weeks, so I get to leave after lunch on Fridays for the whole month. I was talking to Jean-Mathias about maybe taking advantage of those extra hours (since I got paid yesterday) and doing some traveling on the weekends. He suggested Lyon to start, both because it's close and easy to get to on the train and because it's an easy city to get around if you don't have a car. And since I don't, that's important. I looked it up and I can get a train that runs every hour for about twenty euros and be there in about an hour, so maybe I'll go next weekend.

I wonder if Jean-Mathias would like to go with me. I'd ask Pierre, of course, but he's in Bretagne until the middle of the month, and it would be more fun to go with someone than to go by myself.

We aren't playing football on Sunday because too many of the guys are on vacation, so Jean-Mathias and I decided to go hiking on Sunday in the Parc National de la Vanoise. It's a little over an hour from here, but Jean-Mathias said he'd drive us up there, we could hike all day, and I could drive back.

I'm not sure how I feel about driving back. My US driver's license is valid here, so that's not a problem, but there's the whole issue of different rules of the road. I guess it'll be okay since Jean-Mathias will be in the car with me to help if I make any stupid mistakes.

We won't have football next weekend either, so maybe Jean-Mathias will be free to go with me to Lyon. We could find a youth hostel or a cheap hotel and spend our money on good food. Lyon was one of the places the lady on the plane told me I needed to go. And if Jean-Mathias has been there before, he could give me some pointers too.

I guess I'll ask on Sunday and see what he says.

Saturday, August 3

I am so glad I decided to live with a family rather than getting my own apartment. I spent yesterday afternoon and today wandering around the house and then wandering around town with absolutely nothing to do and no one to do it with. At least when the Moreaus are home, I can hang out with Serge and Elodie and watch TV. Watching

TV by myself is no fun because I don't get half the jokes and there's no one to explain them to me.

At least tomorrow I have plans. I should head to church tonight since I won't have time tomorrow.

Monday, August 5

I was too tired last night to do anything but fall in bed when we got back. It was an amazing day, hiking up in the mountains. We carried sandwiches and stuff with us so we wouldn't have to worry about lunch or dinner. Jean-Mathias picked me up early, so we were to the park by around seven thirty. We hiked until it was nearly dark, which was nine thirty, to my amazement. I forget how much farther north we are here. At home, it's dark by eight, maybe eight-thirty this time of year.

The park was amazing, all green and lush with rugged mountains and open fields and wildflowers. I've done the Texas Wildflower Trail more than once, but this was different. You knew these were really wild as opposed to wildflowers planted in strategic locations. Yes, that's cynical, but don't tell me it's not true. Up in the Vanoise, though, everything was natural. There was this lake we hiked around. Jean-Mathias joked that we should jump in and cool off, but neither of us had a change of shorts, and I didn't want to hike the rest of the day in wet underwear. We settled for sitting on a big rock at the edge of the lake and dangling our feet in the water instead. Between that and the breeze, we cooled off pretty fast once we sat down. It might be in the mid 30s (Celsius, of course. I'm having to learn what temperature means what all over again), but with the breeze off the snow-capped mountains and the glacier melt water on our feet, it wasn't as bad as it could have been.

True to his word, Jean-Mathias made me drive home. It was so late that there wasn't much traffic coming down out of the park until we got to the autoroute. And driving on that is easy. It's just like driving on the interstate back home. So we made it home in the appropriate number of pieces. Jean-Mathias dropped me off to get ready for bed and limp into work this morning. I thought I was in pretty good shape, but I'm definitely feeling all the hills today. Fortunately for my pride, Jean-Mathias was walking a little stiffly today too.

The best news, though, is that he's free next weekend to go to Lyon with me, so all I have to do is get through three more nights alone in the house and then I'll have company for a few days. Oh, and Wednesday is David et Jonathan, which means only two nights alone in the house. And Pierre comes home the Friday after that. I don't know that he'll stay at the house, but hopefully I'll get to see him some over that weekend and the next. And not just on the weekends necessarily. We could have dinner together or even go out as long as we didn't stay out too late on a weeknight.

I dreamed in college about having a place of my own, having shared dorm rooms for four years, but now that I have one, I'm finding I don't enjoy it nearly as much as I expected to. Live and learn, I guess.

Jean-Mathias has a friend who lives in Lyon, so he's calling his friend to get recommendations for a place to stay, and then depending on what we find, Jean-Mathias said it might be cheaper to split gas and parking than to pay for two train tickets. If the hotel has parking available. If it doesn't, it's probably cheaper to take the train for the weekend. We'll see what his friend has to say and go from there.

Thursday, August 8

I guess I should start with yesterday since I went to David et Jonathan again. Alexandre's husband Claude was there too last night. Seeing them together was like seeing my parents together. I mean, obviously not exactly the same, but I could see the same devotion and the same affection that I always saw between my parents. Not anything mushy or all kissy and stuff, but in the way they smiled at each other or the way they finished each other's sentences. Like they belong together.

I suppose that's because they do.

It made me all the more determined to find that one day.

I told them a little about meeting Pierre and our two dates. Not about kissing him. It wasn't that kind of evening with that kind of sharing. We did talk some about how I feel about him and how I think he feels about me, and a bit about what I should be entitled to expect from him. It was a little embarrassing not to know, but no one criticized me for it or made me feel bad for asking the questions I did. If anything, they seemed happy I cared enough about myself and my spiritual and emotional well-being to think about these things instead of running blindly into a relationship, or at least into sexual interactions, that I might later regret.

It also made me realize that Pierre and I need to have a long talk before too long. I'm not asking him to marry me or anything, but I want to make sure we have the same expectations. Are we exclusive? Is he open to the idea of a longer-term relationship, not necessarily right this moment, but is that something he wants? Obviously if we go forward from here and find that we don't fit the way we want to, we can end the relationship when that happens, but if he isn't even looking for that, there's no reason for me to start down that road with him. We can still do things together, still have fun and be friends, but I don't go around making out with my friends, and I'm not going to start now.

There's nothing I can do about that, though, until next weekend when he comes home. I have his cell phone, and I might even call him, but I'm not going to have that kind of conversation over the phone. Neither of us needs that kind of stress.

Okay, so that was yesterday in a nutshell. Tomorrow Jean-Mathias and I leave for Lyon. We decided to stay right downtown in the pedestrian center of town, so that means taking the train. The nearest parking lot wasn't close, first of all, and the fees for a weekend would have been more than the cost of two train tickets, and that didn't even count gas (which is even more expensive here than it is at home. It makes me glad I don't have a car!)

I'll take my duffel with me to work. That way we can grab lunch and then catch the one-thirty train to Lyon. That was another eye opener for me. I figured a ticket would be good for one specific train only, like it was on the TGV on the way down here, but Jean-Mathias said that for the regional trains like the one we'll be taking to get to Lyon, the ticket is good for any train, so if we miss the one thirty for whatever reason, we can take the one forty-five or the two forty-five with no problem. We didn't reserve seats or anything since it's an afternoon train and not likely to be full, so we don't even have to worry about that.

Jean-Mathias's friend gave us a huge list of restaurants and clubs to choose from, and of course there's all the other attractions in the city as well. The silk factories, the museums, the archeological digs… Jean-Mathias talked me into getting a Lyon City Card so we can get into everything free instead of having to pay for each attraction separately. I'm looking forward to it, actually. I've gotten plenty of exercise in the past month, but I feel like I haven't done a lot of cultural stuff other than the film retrospective.

Yes, I'm here to work and all that, but I can't imagine living in France for a year without trying to absorb as much of the history and art and architecture and culture as I can. That just seems… a waste of opportunity. I'm not a huge student of art and history, not like Teresa, but that doesn't mean I can't appreciate it. If nothing else, it'll make me feel a little less ignorant when the people around me make these casual references to certain things being built under Louis this or Henri that, which tells everyone else in the room exactly when it was built and gives me absolutely no information at all.

At least if I go on some guided tours of places and notice dates and stuff, I'll get a general sense of what went on when. I hope. I can deal with a lot of things, but feeling ignorant isn't something I'll ever be comfortable with.

Jean-Mathias said we shouldn't plan on going out anywhere fancy, that there was no reason to spend that kind of money when there were plenty of little bistros with amazing food tucked in all over the city, so I'm taking shorts and T-shirts and comfortable shoes. It's supposed to be warm this weekend, and I doubt I'll find any more air conditioning in Lyon than anywhere else. Everyone keeps saying it's just for a few weeks, and so it's simpler to live with the heat than to pay for the expense of installing window units or ducts for central air. After living in Texas all my life, I can't even imagine that, but if it really is only four to six weeks like people say, maybe it does make sense. At home, we have the air on from April through October if we're lucky. If we're not, it's March through November.

It's supposed to be in the upper twenties or low thirties again, which is only the mid to upper 80s at home, but it cools off significantly at night and that helps. Shorts and T-shirts should be fine, although I've already learned to toss in a sweater just in case. It <u>does</u> cool off in the evenings. I should finish packing and then go to bed. I'll write tomorrow night from Lyon.

Friday, August 9

We're in Lyon. Jean-Mathias decided he wanted a shower before dinner, so I'm sitting at the balcony/hallway outside our hotel room overlooking the courtyard. I don't really know how to describe it. It's not like a motel at home with the tacky metal stairs. The hotel was an old house or maybe an old apartment building, but like, really old. Sixteenth century old, so I guess it wouldn't have been apartments so much as separate little family dwellings all in one building. Anyway, the stairs are mostly inside and then they give out onto these open walkways at random intervals, each one going to two or three doors, and all of it decorated with, or built with, probably, the same old wooden beams like in my room in Grenoble. A picture would be much easier than trying to describe the hotel, but even if I took a photo, I can't get it here in the journal. I'll just have to make a note on the picture when I save it to my computer that tags it with my entry from today, so when I look at this in ten years, I'll be able to find the hotel picture again.

There, picture taken.

So anyway, we got in today around three, no problems with the train, dropped off our bags, and headed out for a guided tour of the city. Jean-Mathias assured me they weren't just for tourists, that he likes to go on the one in Grenoble from time to time just to remind himself of the richness of his city.

So we got an overview of the city and its history and I have a much better idea of where things are and what our options are as far as museums and attractions are concerned. I'm especially interested in the Gallo-Roman stuff and the silk making. I had no idea before coming to France that Lyon was the silk capital of Europe. I mean, I guess it makes sense that the Silk Road had to end somewhere, but I didn't know it was here.

Tonight, though, we're going in search of Lyonnais delicacies. No andouillette for me, but Jean-Mathias has been raving about the quenelles and all the other kinds of sausages besides the andouillette. And the wine. I'm still a little nervous about my lack of experience, but he promised he'd choose a bottle for us that I'd like.

He's ready to go.

Sunday, August 11

We're on our way back to Grenoble. The train's a little bumpy so if my handwriting is worse than usual, that's why. Jean-Mathias is napping so I don't feel rude about writing while we're together instead of waiting until tonight.

We had a blast this weekend. I'm so glad he was free to go with me because I would have missed so much if I'd been by myself. Even if I'd visited all the same places, I wouldn't have had his insight into what it all meant. Not to mention his expertise in finding little "hole-in-the-wall" bistros to eat. And in choosing wine. We drank a lot of rosé wine this weekend in deference to the heat. Jean-Mathias explained that red wine is heavier and so when it's hot, it's better to drink white wine or rosé. Given the sausage we ate all weekend, the rosé was a better choice.

I'm not looking forward to going back to an empty house again tonight after spending the weekend with Jean-Mathias. And I've got another three weeks of this. Pierre will be home on Friday, though, so maybe it won't be quite so bad after he gets back. He's never stayed at the house full-time since I've been here, but even if I got to see him a couple of times a week, that would be better than the house being completely empty.

This might be bad. This is the first time all weekend I've thought about Pierre and missing him. I was having too much fun to think about him. I guess that's another question to store up for the next David et Jonathan. Obviously I'm allowed to have a weekend with friends instead of with Pierre, especially when he's out of town already, but should I have thought about him more? Or maybe called him at some point? It seemed rude to do that with Jean-Mathias around. He knows about Pierre, of course, but the weekend was my idea and it seems awkward to then excuse myself to call someone else, like Jean-Mathias's company wasn't enough. Except, obviously it was since I didn't think about Pierre until now. Not even when Jean-Mathias was talking about wine.

I'll call Pierre when I get back to the house tonight. That way he'll know I'm thinking about him and that I miss him. And maybe we can make plans for next weekend.

Yeah, I'll do that.

I'm home from church (thanks goodness for evening services!) and I just got off the phone with Pierre. He sounded… distracted, so I didn't talk for long, but he promised to come by the house Friday night so we could do something. Not the most concrete of plans, but it's better than nothing, I suppose. I tried not to call at dinnertime or anything, but that doesn't mean they weren't in the middle of something as a family. And I didn't have a suggestion of something to do this time for him to agree or disagree with, so he might want time to think up something fun.

I'm not going to worry about this. This is ridiculous. I'm closing my journal and going to bed.

Tuesday, August 13

After moping around by myself Sunday and Monday nights, I was in a bad mood today at work, and as we were leaving, Jean-Mathias asked me what was wrong. So I told him about the empty house and how depressing that was. I felt a bit like a dweeb for saying anything, but he did ask. He laughed at me and told me to stop sulking and come to the market with him. We'd find something for dinner and throw it together at his place. That way I could have a few more hours before I had to be in an empty house. I felt kind of bad that he felt obliged to invite me over, but we had such a good time (at least I did) that I can't regret it. Dinner wasn't anything fancy. Breaded pork chops, steamed asparagus with Béarnaise sauce, and the ever-present salad and cheese courses. It wasn't about the meal anyway. It was about the company.

Jean-Mathias now knows how absolutely hopeless I am in the kitchen, but I'm a little less hopeless after tonight. Instead of throwing up his hands, he showed me what to do and then made sure I did it right. I actually made the salad dressing all by myself after he told me how. Okay, fine, if you get the right proportions, mixing mustard, red wine vinegar, and olive oil isn't difficult, but even so, I did it. You'd think as much chemistry as I took in college, I'd be better at this whole cooking thing, but I guess it's lack of experience. Mom doesn't share her kitchen with anyone and I ate in the cafeteria in college. And now I eat at the Moreaus or in a café for lunch.

And as we cooked and ate, we talked. Comfortable, casual conversation. It felt really good. Like I've really made a friend I'll keep in touch with even after this year is over.

Isn't that the way I'm supposed to feel about Pierre?

I hate to say that I don't, but I don't. Of course, I don't see him as often. I see Jean-Mathias every day at work if nothing else. Plus football on the weekends when we have it. Jean-Mathias said it would start back up in September when everyone got back from vacation. He asked if I wanted to plan something for this weekend so we could get some exercise in, but I told him Pierre would be back in town and I didn't want to make plans until I'd talked to him.

Jean-Mathias seemed a little disappointed, but he said it was no big deal and to call him if I had some free time and wanted to go for a run or a swim or anything like that.

Could he be as lonely as I am with all his other friends out of town? I guess it's possible. Maybe I should invite him to come with me to the Pole Étudiant tomorrow night. We've never really discussed church or anything like that, but we've only spent two Sunday mornings together. I didn't think about it when we went hiking because I'd gone to church the night before, and we were so busy in Lyon that I didn't think about it in the morning and we were home in time. Needless to say I went to church when we got back since it wasn't all that late. Maybe he did the same thing.

I guess I'll ask him and see. It's not like his answer would change our friendship. He's entitled to his beliefs and his expression of them even if they aren't the same as mine. But he might want to go. It's not like everyone at the Pole Étudiant shares the exact same beliefs anyway. There's a huge spectrum of conservative to liberal interpretations of the topics we've discussed so far, which makes for some really interesting, eye-opening conversations. And if Jean-

Mathias comes once and it isn't for him, that's still one evening he hasn't spent alone. If he really is as lonely as I've been with everyone out of town, he might appreciate the chance.

I'll mention it tomorrow and see if he wants to come. It's not quite as nice an invitation as him inviting me to his apartment for dinner, but it's the best I've got, at least for tomorrow. Although even then, I'm not sure I'd invite him to the Moreaus' house without asking them first.

Thursday, August 15

Pierre gets home tomorrow. He called again tonight to confirm that he'd meet me at his parents' house as soon as he gets in, which should be soon after four. I get off at noon since it's Friday, so I'll probably go for a long swim after lunch to pass the time. I have to do something. If I sit at the house waiting for him, I'll go crazy with watching the numbers change on the clock.

In other news, Jean-Mathias didn't come with me last night to Pole Étudiant because he'd promised his mother and sister he'd have dinner with them to talk about wedding plans, but he seemed in interested in possibly coming another week. Next week is his vacation (he's going to Rome, lucky guy!), but maybe the week after that. The crowd was really thin last night anyway, so it wouldn't have been the best introduction for him to the group. It was still interesting. Maybe even more interesting. We didn't have a set topic because of it being August, so instead it turned into a discussion of the letter from Paul which was the one on love. "Love is patient, love is kind. It does not envy, it does not boast, it is not proud. It is not rude, it is not self-seeking, it is not easily angered, it keeps no record of wrongs. Love does not delight in evil but rejoices with the truth. Love bears all things, believes all things, hopes all things, endures all things. Love never fails. But where there are prophecies, they will cease; where there are tongues, they will be stilled; where there is knowledge, it will pass away. For we know in part and we prophesy in part, but when perfection comes, the imperfect disappears. And now these three remain: faith, hope and love. But the greatest of these is love."

There aren't a lot of Bible verses I can quote verbatim, but that's one of them. Well, it's more than a single verse, but that's beside the point. Those words have always resonated with me to the depths of my soul. Even Paul, as homophobic as he could be (yes, I know, he was a product of his society and surrounded by some very specific situations that led to his attitudes), doesn't define love here. He simply says love. And if my love is for another man but is still the beautiful, pure love Paul describes, then it is love, and it endures, and it is great. Not in the "gee that's great" kind of way but in the "the greatest of these is love" way.

Now I simply have to hold onto that faith until I find my love.

See what I mean about an interesting discussion? And the best part? I wasn't the one who brought up the issue of how we define love. Cristian, an exchange student from Spain, brought it up, almost like he was challenging the people there to tell him his love for his boyfriend, who he plans to marry when he returns to Spain after his semester in France, was wrong. Nobody blinked an eye. If he loves his fiancé that much, then it's love the same as Anne and her fiancé.

It gives me such hope.

I truly feared I wouldn't ever find a way to be true to myself and to my faith, and I feared for my sanity if I couldn't balance them because the two most basic tenets of my life should not be in conflict. I am gay and I am Christian. They shouldn't be mutually exclusive. Last night they weren't.

My mother would occasionally make a comment about God showing up and showing off when something went so much better than planned or expected, when something bordering on miraculous occurred. I'm pretty sure the last two months for me have been exactly that.

And on that note, I think I'll go to bed. I want to be rested for whatever Pierre suggests for tomorrow night.

Saturday, August 17

I got in too late last night to write, so I'll write this morning and then again tonight if there's anything to add. Pierre got in early, to my surprise, so he was at the house when I got home from swimming. He suggested we go to Le Loungta, a gay and lesbian bar. They have themes on the weekends, and in honor of it being vacation time, they did a Caribbean theme last night. It was fun, but definitely not a quiet night at home. We spent the entire evening in each other's company without me feeling like we spent any time together.

I feel awful writing that. Pierre wanted to do something fun and wanted to share it with me. And it was fun. The food was good and the music was very reggae, steel-drum style, very festive. The kind of music that makes it impossible to sit still. Now if only I were a better dancer. I'm not hopeless, but I could see Pierre losing patience with me at times. He ended up dancing with other people as much as he danced with me.

I guess I should be happy he didn't disappear into the restroom like I saw some other couples doing. He came with me, he ate dinner with me, and he left with me. And he did dance with me some, and so did some of the other guys. They were all much more patient with me than my date. I think maybe dancing should not be on our list of things to do on a date. Not if Pierre is going to dance with someone else half the time.

He came in when we got back to the house and we talked for a bit. He shared some funny stories about his brother and sister and listened to me talk about work. He wasn't interested in hearing about anything related to Jean-Mathias, though. I think he might have been jealous. I tried to tell him there was no reason, but then he got all defensive and didn't want to talk about it anymore. So we ended up making out on the couch. It got kind of hot and heavy there for a bit, but just about the time I started to get uncomfortable, Pierre backed off and went back to soft kisses.

I know sex is a part of a healthy, loving, long-term relationship, but I'm not ready to make that commitment yet. I don't know whether

Pierre agrees with me on that or whether he simply realized I was ready to bolt and so chilled as a way to keep me on the couch with him. It's something I'll have to figure out eventually. He agreed to my suggestion of going biking this afternoon. Serge said I could use his bike if he wasn't using it, and since he's gone for the whole month, I don't think he'll be using it. I haven't taken it out yet since I've been busy doing other things, but this way Pierre and I are doing something that doesn't involve a club and drinking, and I'm getting some exercise at the same time since we aren't playing football tomorrow.

Maybe I'll invite Pierre to church with me in the morning too. For now, though, I need to get something to eat and wash the sweat and cigarette smell off me from last night. Yes, I know, kind of pointless to wash the sweat off when I'm getting ready to spend the afternoon biking in thirty degree weather (nearly 90 at home), but I'd like to start the day clean. I can always shower again tonight when we get home.

I'm a little worried, I have to admit. I like Pierre, and I enjoy our time together, but I'm not sure we want the same things out of our relationship or that we have enough of the same priorities to make things work between us for more than a few, fun dates.

While we were out riding today (Grenoble has some beautiful bike trails. I have to do that again.), I mentioned church tomorrow to Pierre, just wondering if he'd like to go with me. He laughed and said he'd have too much of a hangover to get up at some ungodly hour to go to church.

Mass is at ten thirty. That isn't all that early, but I thought I'd try again, so I mentioned evening Mass. It's not until seven thirty. He'd be recovered by then. He looked at me seriously and said he hadn't set foot in a church in ten years and had no intention of changing that in the next ten, unless it was to attend the wedding of a friend.

I can't even imagine living that way. What does he do when he has doubts or decisions to make? Where does he go for wisdom and counsel?

I don't know the answers for him, and maybe I'm not meant to. I probably could live with that if I thought he respected my choices in going to church and having a spiritual life. I'd prefer to share that with my partner, but I think I could accept not sharing it as long as he respected my right to make my own choices. Pierre's reaction felt derisive, and I can't live with that. Not to mention the whole hangover thing when we hadn't planned on going out tonight as far as I knew. It makes me wonder who he's going out with besides me and what they're doing.

I don't want to fight with Pierre over it, in part because I don't want to lose my living situation. Staying here if we'd had a big fight would be awkward, and moving would probably mean living by myself, which I've learned this month is not for me.

He said he'd come by Monday after work. I'll talk to him then and see if I can explain my feelings without hurting his.

Can I go back to being twelve? Life was simple then.

Monday, August 19

I'm not sure if I should be relieved or angry right now. Maybe I should be both.

Pierre called about an hour ago. He said he wasn't going to come over tonight after all because he didn't think we wanted the same things out of a relationship. He said he wasn't ready to get all heavy and serious, that he was still in college, with at least one more year to go, but probably a master's degree after that, and that he was still having fun, not trying to settle down. He promised we'd still see each other when he came to eat at his parents' house, but he didn't think we should go out anymore, at least not alone.

I should be relieved it wasn't any big scene since I was planning on saying the same thing to him. After all, if it's a mutual decision, there shouldn't need to be any drama. So I'm not sure why I'm so annoyed. Because he said it first? That's beyond petty. He wasn't cruel about it, and he's certainly right that we're looking for different things. I want a partner. A husband. He doesn't right now. There's nothing wrong with that. I wouldn't have wanted one a year ago. I needed to focus on my studies then, and he needs to do that now. And he was honest enough not to claim that as his only reason. I don't agree with "playing the field" the way a lot of people do before they get married. If I'm dating someone, I want it to be someone I can envision building a life with. But my choices don't have to be Pierre's. He's entitled to make his own path, wherever that leads him, and I hope he finds happiness in those choices.

Or maybe I'm annoyed because he did it over the phone. People don't realize how hard it is to talk on the phone when you're talking in a language not your own. I practice conversations in my head before I pick up the phone because there aren't any cues other than the words themselves. When you're standing next to someone, you can see their facial expressions, their gestures, etc., but on the phone, you don't have any of that, and you have static on the line sometimes too, which only makes it worse. It's not the challenge of the conversation, though. It's the fact that he didn't have enough guts to look me in the face and tell me it was over. That's what rankles most.

I'll get over it. It's not like I had time to fall in love with him. It's just disappointing that I misjudged the situation so badly my first time out. I mean, sure, it could have been worse. He could have been the type to pressure me into having sex on the first date or something like that. But I thought by finding someone my own age, I'd find someone at the same stage I was at, ready to start finding someone to build a life with. Maybe that was my mistake. Mom always said I was older than my years. Maybe I need to find someone a little older than I am, someone who's done sowing his wild oats or whatever you want to call it. I might have more luck with that.

Now I have to figure out how to fill my time until Jean-Mathias gets back. I'd planned on spending it with Pierre, but that's obviously not an option now.

I wonder if I need to find another place to live. I hope not. I guess I'll see how it goes when the Moreaus get back and when Pierre comes over for dinner the first time. If it's miserably awkward, I can always look for a new place then.

Friday, August 23

Talk about a shitty week. Jean-Mathias is out of town. The only other tech in the lab is someone I barely know. Pierre hasn't been around (no big surprise there, but I'd originally expected us to spend the week together). The Moreaus don't get back for another week. And I have nothing to do this weekend.

I kept thinking about Jean-Mathias telling me about going on the guided tour of Grenoble even though he's lived here all his life, so I took the tour this afternoon. It was really interesting. I knew Grenoble was an old city, but I didn't realize it dated to pre-Roman times. Nor did I realize how incredibly active the Résistance was here during World War II. I did know that the heir to the French throne was called le Dauphin because of the treaty that incorporated this area into France proper, but I think that was the only thing I heard today that I already knew. No, that's not true. I knew about the Olympics in 1968, although I wouldn't have been able to tell you what year. The tour didn't include a ride on Les Bulles up to the Bastille, but the guide told us all about the fortifications and their role in the city's development. I think tomorrow I'll go for a ride and wander around to get a better feel for them. She also raved about the musée de Grenoble, the art museum. That's something else I could do this weekend. Maybe the museum will have an audio tour. Even if it costs a little extra, I think it would be worth it the first time so I know what I'm seeing. If I go back another time, I can skip it then.

Saturday, August 24

Another day of exploring Grenoble. I enjoyed it, but I think I'd have enjoyed it more with someone. Maybe the next time I decide to do that, I'll invite Jean-Mathias along or see if someone from the Pole Étudiant wants to go.

I went up to the Bastille and wandered the fortifications and all the old gates and tunnels. It was fascinating to see all the old construction and how solid it still is. Some of those walls and guardhouses date from the eleventh and twelfth centuries. I mean, I'm sure they've been shored up and all, but you certainly can't tell it to look at them.

I did that this morning while it was still relatively cool. Then this afternoon I went to the museum. They did have an audio tour, so I got that for a start, and then I simply wandered. I actually ended up talking to one of the curators. I heard him answering someone else's question, so I asked him one of mine as well, and we got to talking. His name was Yves Richard. We actually ended up talking until the museum closed. He knows so much about art and history. It was humbling, honestly, to have to admit my ignorance, but he was kind about it. He didn't make me feel like it was anything to be ashamed of. In fact, when I apologized at one point for all my questions, he said there was nothing wrong with admitting you didn't know something when you were obviously trying to learn more about the subject. The problem was in being willfully ignorant and doing nothing about it.

I like that philosophy. Quite a bit, actually. There's no shame in not having been exposed to it. The shame is in not learning something when we are exposed to it.

I know it sounds odd, but as the museum was closing (and we were still talking), Yves said if I didn't mind waiting a few minutes for him to make sure everything was closed, he'd love to continue our conversation. We ended up going to a café near the museum to talk, and coffee turned into dinner.

Yves suggested I come back next weekend and he'll take me on a behind-the-scenes visit of the museum. I couldn't say no to that! Not after I learned so much just from the public face of the museum.

I'm going to get online tomorrow and look up some art history stuff, some technical terms and that kind of thing. I know a few things from my course in college, although that was four years ago now, but I never learned those terms in French, and some of what Yves said went over my head.

Now I just have to fill my time until next Saturday. I didn't think to suggest Friday afternoon.

Tomorrow I have church in the morning, and then I figured I'd go to the pool and swim for a while, and then maybe take Serge's bike back out along the trails. Last weekend's breakup aside, the biking was a lot of fun. I'll take my phone with me just in case since I'll be by myself. Jean-Mathias gets home tomorrow, but I doubt he'll be home before late. I'll see him at work on Monday, though, so I can catch him up on everything with Pierre and tell him about meeting Yves.

Monday, August 26

Jean-Mathias thinks Yves was hitting on me at the museum.

I think he's full of it because what would a man like that see in me, assuming for one minute that he's gay? And since I didn't have any indication that he was, that changes the likelihood from slim to none.

I'll take my behind-the-scenes tour on Saturday. That will be the end of it, and Jean-Mathias can stuff it.

In the meantime, he's going to come with me to Pole Étudiant on Wednesday. How cool is that? I can't wait to introduce him to everyone there. There wasn't a theme announced last week for this Wednesday, so it might end up being another open discussion. Sometimes I think I like those best. The themes are interesting, but someone is there with a set agenda of points to discuss. When the discussions stem from the readings and go where they take us, it seems more natural. More genuine. Of course that's easier with a group of ten or fifteen than with a group of forty or fifty, which is why they usually have a plan. I get that. I just like the small group setting.

Paolo teased us today about me moping around last week without Jean-Mathias. We laughed, but I didn't realize how true it was until I got to thinking about it. He's definitely taken on best-friend status, which is beyond awesome because I need someone to just be with, no stress, no worries, no demands. I'd hoped maybe Pierre would give me that (with a little romance thrown in), but that didn't work out. I haven't given up. It's only the end of August. I still have most of the year left, and of course, there's the rest of my life once I get back to Texas and start graduate school.

It's amazingly easy to forget that I'm going home at the end of the year. Everything feels so comfortable, even after only two months. I'm so much more fluent than I ever imagined possible. Not native yet. I still make mistakes or run across things I don't know how to say, like yesterday at the museum with Yves, but I no longer feel like I'm struggling to understand simple sentences or to get my point across. And that will only get better as time goes on. By the end of May, I bet I won't have to think about any but the newest, most technical situations. I doubt I'll lose my accent completely, but that isn't my goal anyway. My goal is to be functional. I'd say I'm already 80% there.

Okay, time for bed. I'll write more later.

Tuesday, August 27

I dreamed in French last night! Here I was saying, just yesterday, that I could tell my fluency was improving, and now I've dreamt in French. That's, like, the ultimate threshold to fluency because that's your subconscious creating language for you without your conscious mind interfering. I am so stoked. I can't wait to tell Jean-Mathias. He'll probably laugh at me for being such a dork, but it's a milestone for me.

Have to get ready for work now.

Jean-Mathias not only didn't laugh, he bought lunch today to celebrate. It was still sandwiches at our café, but he treated me. It was a much appreciated gesture.

And he came to the pool with me tonight after work.

I probably shouldn't have let myself notice since he's my friend and all, but wow, he's built. I hadn't really thought about it until now. I mean, we shared a room at the gîte and in Lyon, but it's not like he walked around in just a pair of Speedos either time.

Jean-Mathias in Speedos is a sight to behold. I only hope I managed to hide the drool.

I am not supposed to be thinking about my friend, my straight friend, this way. Not cool at all.

I have to get this out of my system before work tomorrow or I'll never be able to look him in the eye. Of course, if I do the obvious and even the slightest image of him in a Speedo crosses my mind while I'm doing it, that'll make it even harder to look him in the eye. I think the thing to do is just go to sleep. I'll deal with the rest another time.

Thursday, August 29

I managed to look Jean-Mathias in the eye when I got to work yesterday, and once we were at our benches working, laughing and talking like usual, all the uncomfortable tension in my gut faded. So he's attractive. So I noticed. No big deal. I'm human. I'm allowed to appreciate beauty when I see it, even if it's beauty that's untouchable. And appreciating his beauty doesn't have to have any repercussions on our friendship.

We went straight from work to the Pole Étudiant last night. Jean-Mathias insisted on driving me so I wouldn't have to take the bus. I think he had a really good time. He dropped me off afterward, and we talked quite a bit about the group and the evening on the way home. We disagreed on some things, but it isn't about agreeing. It's about having the discussion. Why couldn't Pierre see that?

Oh well. Water under the bridge.

Today was pretty much uneventful. Work, lunch, work, swimming (without Jean-Mathias this time), dinner.

Tomorrow is our last half-day Friday. I haven't decided what I'll do with the extra hours. Maybe I should do laundry before the Moreaus get home this weekend since I imagine they'll have a ton to do before they go back to work on Monday.

I think Serge and Elodie start school soon too. I can't remember when exactly Mme Moreau said, but I know it was early September. Once that happens, I'll have to talk with them about when they'd want help with their English, whether they'd want to set up a schedule or just ask me for help when they need it. They'll learn more if we set up a schedule and spend an hour or two a week talking in English, even if it's about what we had for dinner, but I've heard that French high school students work far harder than their American counterparts, so I don't know how realistic that would be. Any weeknight but Wednesday would work for me since I'm not likely to be traveling during the week, with work and all. I just don't know what else they have going on besides school. Do they have extracurricular activities like we do?

I guess I'll find out.

Saturday, August 31

The Moreaus are home. I'm glad I did laundry yesterday because there's a month's worth of dirty laundry spread all over the buanderie (their laundry room). Mme Moreau asked about Pierre, and I simply replied I hadn't seen him since the weekend he got back to Grenoble. She seemed a little surprised, but that was it, so I'm hoping that means I won't have to move.

I went back to the museum today to see Yves, despite Jean-Mathias's warnings. I really don't think there's anything to be concerned about. He showed me around the museum, the public side as well as the workshops in the back where they restore paintings and prepare new acquisitions for display. We talked for several hours. There's a Sunday with the Arts next weekend (actually every weekend in September) and Yves suggested I attend. He said he thought I'd find it interesting given our conversations. It's only three euros. I asked if he'd be there, and he said yes.

Maybe Jean-Mathias is right and he is flirting with me. Nothing like Pierre, but then Yves is nothing like Pierre so I suppose it's logical that he'd flirt (if that's what he's doing) differently.

The only problem with going to the Sunday with the Arts is that I'd miss football. Jean-Mathias already told me everyone would be back in town and ready to play tomorrow, so that means next weekend as well. Not that everyone is there every weekend. It's not like it's a league or anything, but even so, it feels odd to be in town and do something else. The program isn't something I have to RSVP for, so I can always see how I feel on Sunday. Or maybe I could see if Jean-Mathias wants to do something on Saturday. That way I'm not completely blowing him off for the weekend. I don't know if he'll go to Pole Étudiant this week, but I won't even be there if he does because it's the first Wednesday of the month, and he'd have no interest in going to David et Jonathan with me.

I'll just have to see how things go, I guess. I really like Yves, and it wasn't a problem to miss football when I spent the weekend with Pierre at the vineyard. I'm not sure why this feels different then. Maybe because I get the feeling Jean-Mathias doesn't approve of Yves the way he seemed to approve of Pierre, or at least the idea of Pierre since they didn't actually meet.

That doesn't make a whole lot of sense to me, honestly. I mean, Yves is a professional, well established in his career. He's mature and responsible and far more likely to want what I want out of life than someone like Pierre who's still in college and not ready to settle down. Not that Yves and I have talked about anything like that. I don't know him that well yet. I'm just saying that in general, he's a better candidate for a relationship than Pierre was.

And if I'm wrong, if all I end up getting out of it is an education in the arts, I figure I still come out ahead.

Wednesday, September 4

Have I really already been here for over two full months? Where does the time go? Today was la rentrée, the first day of classes, so Serge and Elodie got home all excited (or nervous) about their new classes, new teachers, and all that. Elodie is especially worried because her English teacher has a reputation for being impossible to please. I told her we'd find a way, just not tonight since I have David et Jonathan.

I had to come home to get the salad I made for dinner tonight. I was afraid if I took it to work with me and then to the café where I usually hang out until it's time to gather, it would end up wilted or spoiled. I'm not anything special as a cook, but I have enough pride to want to bring something nice within my limitations.

It's about time to go. I probably won't write tonight when I get back, but I will tomorrow.

Sunday, September 8

Okay, so I lied. I didn't write on Thursday after all, and now it's Sunday. Jean-Mathias had plans already for yesterday, so I haven't seen him at all this weekend. I decided to go to the Sunday with the Arts instead of to football. I'll play football next weekend.

Yves seemed pleased to see me, staying at my side as much as his role in the presentation would allow. And then after it was over, he invited me for coffee again. And over coffee, he asked if I'd like to go to a reception to raise money for the museum on Thursday night. As his date.

I apparently have no gaydar because I really didn't think he was interested in me that way. Jean-Mathias hasn't even met Yves and he picked up on it, but I seem doomed to be clueless.

I warned Yves not to expect me to be witty or anything like that since my French was still only passable, despite the improvements I've made since I've been here.

He assured me I would be fine and that he'd be proud to have me at his side, "a handsome young man like you."

I don't see it when I look in the mirror. Brownish hair that defies any single color. Blue eyes. Regular features. I mean, I know I'm not ugly or anything, but I don't think of myself as being particularly handsome. Does anyone, though, unless it's their job in some respect? I take the time to make sure I'm neat, that my hair is brushed, my clothes clean, that sort of thing, but that's all the concern I've ever taken with my appearance. I suppose that old adage about beauty being in the eye of the beholder is true.

So now I have to figure out what to wear to a reception on Thursday night. Fortunately I brought all my good shirts, thinking I'd need them for work. Surely I'll have something that works.

Monday, September 9

Jean-Mathias is annoyed at me.

I'm not really sure why. He knew I wouldn't be at football yesterday, and I promised I'd be there next week. I'm not sure he believes me, though. I told him about Yves, about the presentation yesterday and about Thursday night. He told me I was making a mistake, but it's my mistake to make, which is what I told him.

I don't think he liked that answer very much, but what else am I supposed to say? I like Yves. I've enjoyed our conversations. I've enjoyed learning about art. I like the idea of going to something classy like this reception. Not that I don't also like the traveling Jean-Mathias and I have done, but we can do that any time. I may never get another invitation to a reception like this one, here or at home.

Besides, it's just a reception. It's not like Yves asked me to go away with him for the weekend or anything like that. And even if he did, I've gone away with Jean-Mathias for the weekend twice and Pierre once. There's nothing wrong with that.

Oh, this is pointless. It's my life and I already know what I'm going to do. I don't have to justify my choices to Jean-Mathias, and I don't have to justify them here just because he questioned them. Yes, he's my friend, but I am the arbiter of my life, not him.

Thursday, September 12

My date with Yves is tonight. I'm so nervous I woke up an hour early this morning to make sure everything was ready. Not sure what I thought I needed to get ready an hour early, but I'm too awake to go back to bed.

Jean-Mathias didn't come to Pole Étudiant last night, but apparently he went last week while I was at David et Jonathan because several people asked me where he was last night. I don't know if he had other plans or if he was avoiding me. We didn't eat lunch together Tuesday or yesterday, the first time we've both been at work and not had lunch together since I started working in Dr. Besson's lab. I'm torn between apologizing (not that I know what for) and not saying anything. He's the one who left without me both days. I wasn't happy with his opinion, but it's still his opinion, not a reason to stop talking to each other.

Maybe if I show up for football on Sunday like I promised, he'll start talking to me again. First, though, I have a date tonight. I have my suit laid out and my shirt pressed. I should have time to get home and shower quickly before it's time to leave to meet Yves at the reception. He said he'd gladly bring me home after it was over but that he wouldn't be able to pick me up beforehand because he'd have to get everything ready. I don't mind taking the bus. The heat has broken somewhat the past couple of days, so it's no longer unpleasant to be outside.

Now I just have to get through work today before I can go enjoy myself tonight.

Friday, September 13

I had a great time last night. Yves was wonderful company, keeping me at his side and introducing me to everyone over the course of the evening. It was very posh, a champagne reception with waiters walking around with trays of different hors d'oeuvres. (I hope I spelled that right. You'd think I'd know how to spell it since it's a French word, but I'm never sure I'm right.) I met the mayor of Grenoble. I know, he's a man like anyone else, but at the moment, he's a prominent man, and I'm just an American on a work visa.

The reception was held at Couvent Ste. Cécile, an old convent that's been converted into a meeting hall. When I say converted, I really mean its purpose has changed because as far as I can tell, the building itself is still the same seventeenth century architecture as everything around it. It certainly made for a stunning setting.

I do kind of wish the reception had been tonight instead of last night. It was after midnight when Yves finally dropped me off at the house, and getting up this morning was a challenge. He asked if he'd see me Sunday at the next Sunday with the Arts, but I told him I couldn't make it this week. He seemed disappointed, but I told him I had a prior commitment and he accepted that. He suggested we have dinner on Tuesday instead since that's his day off. I saw no reason to say no.

He didn't kiss me goodnight, but I think he wanted to. Instead he stroked his finger down my cheek. How is it that such a simple caress left me aching for more half the night? Pierre sometimes left me feeling that way, but it took a whole lot more than touching my cheek.

Jean-Mathias asked me how my date went when I came in this morning. I told him I'd tell him all about it at lunch if he wanted to know.

He gave me this odd half-smile and said okay. Lunch was a little awkward, especially when I told him about having dinner with Yves last night, but I also told him I'd turned down an invitation for Sunday so I could come play football. He told me I didn't need to do that, but I think I do. Jean-Mathias is my friend, and that's important too.

Elodie has her first English paper due on Monday, so I promised I'd spend tomorrow helping her with it. I don't know if that will take all day, but I haven't planned anything else, just in case it does. If I end up with extra time, maybe I'll go to the pool or borrow Serge's bike again (if he isn't using it).

Tuesday, September 17

Um, wow.

That's about all I can say at this point. I keep trying to put my thoughts in some semblance of order and I keep failing spectacularly.

So yeah, wow.

Maybe tomorrow I'll actually be coherent.

Wednesday, September 18

Okay, yesterday's entry is plain old embarrassing. If it filled a page, I'd just tear the page out, but it's got part of Friday's entry on it too, and I don't want to lose that. I suppose I could recopy it onto the next page, but maybe it's better to keep the entry, just to remind myself of how I felt yesterday.

So, now that I'm capable of something other than babbling, Yves and I went to dinner last night at a very nice restaurant, the kind of place I wouldn't go in by myself. The food was delicious, easily the best meal I've had since I've been here, and that includes Pierre's birthday dinner. After we were finished, Yves drove us out to the Jardin de Ville, and we walked around for a bit, talking some, but mostly just being together. After a couple of minutes, he stopped and pulled me into his arms with that same stroke down my cheek that he used last week, the one that tied my insides in knots.

And then he kissed me.

There is no way those five little words can sum up what happened last night, but I don't know any others. All I know is that kissing Yves is nothing at all like kissing Pierre. With Pierre, it was sweet and tender and light. There's nothing wrong with that. I'm not sure I'd have wanted my first kiss to be any different than it was. With Yves, though, it was all heavy and wild and claiming. He kisses like he knows what he wants and intends to get it. It's a little scary, but incredibly arousing at the same time because I'm what he wants.

My head was spinning by the time we left the park, and at every red light, he leaned over and kissed me again so that my head was still spinning when he dropped me off at the house. He didn't grope me or anything, but he did pull me close enough against him that I could feel how hard he was in his pants too, like he was showing me my feelings were returned and promising more at a later date.

I came upstairs and wrote last night's babble, but I couldn't sleep. I, um, God, I can't even make myself write it. I jerked off last night to the memory of Yves kissing me. And now, thinking about it, I'm ready to go again. I don't have time because I have to get ready for work, but I have a feeling that will be my favorite fantasy for quite some time.

Unless, of course, Yves gives me new memories to replace this one.

I went to Pole Étudiant tonight. Jean-Mathias came as well, but I ended up leaving early. My head is pounding and my stomach hurts. I think I'm coming down with something. Jean-Mathias brought me home so I wouldn't have to deal with the buses and the waiting, which I really appreciated. He gave me his phone number and told me to call him if I couldn't come in to work tomorrow and needed him to do anything with any of my experiments. I hope I'll feel better in the morning, but if I don't, it'll be a load off my mind not to worry about the gel I set to run overnight right before I left today. I won't ask Jean-Mathias to analyze the data for me. If he'll stop it running and put it in the fridge, I can deal with it when I come back. Assuming I don't feel well enough to go to work tomorrow.

I don't want to be sick. I hate being sick.

Thursday, September 19

I'm sick.

I spent most of last night throwing up.

Mme Moreau called her family doctor, who came to the house to see me. I couldn't believe it. Not that getting to the doctor's office would have been very easy, but I didn't know doctors still made house calls. I have a stomach virus. He gave me a shot for the nausea and told me to get lots of rest and drink plenty of fluids. So now my ass hurts from the shot and I have to get up every fifteen minutes to go to the bathroom because every time I finish a glass of water, Mme Moreau brings me another one. I'm not sure how she knows I've finished, but she always does.

At least I'm not throwing up at the moment. I did manage to call Jean-Mathias, and he promised he'd take care of the gel for me. Fortunately nothing else I have going is time sensitive. Dealing with it tomorrow or, more likely, Monday won't make a difference.

I had to call Yves and cancel our plans for tomorrow night too. Even if the drowsiness from the shot has worn off, I won't be up for a big dinner out with his colleagues from Vienna who are in town to help set up a visiting exhibit from a museum there. He sounded a little put out, but what can I do? I didn't ask to get sick. He promised to call after the Viennese curators leave to make plans for something else.

I imagine this means no football on Sunday either. Oh well, at least Jean-Mathias won't be annoyed at me for missing when I'm sick.

That isn't fair. He wasn't really annoyed at me for missing two weeks ago. He's just worried that Yves isn't a good choice for me. I disagree, and we've agreed to leave it at that. I won't make him listen to all the details and he won't make snarky comments about cradle robbers or anything like that.

Since I don't have him to talk about Yves to, I was thinking I might contact Alexandre at David et Jonathan to see if he could arrange something like a counseling session with someone there, to give me someone to bounce ideas off of. I have a feeling I'm in way over my head here. Not that that's a bad thing. I'm kind of in over my head with pretty much anything at this point, but without someone to talk to, I'm likely to flounder. I'd love to meet with Alexandre or his husband since they actually have what I hope to have someday, but honestly, anyone who isn't fresh out of the closet probably has some wisdom to share.

The medicine is making me sleepy again. I'm going to sleep for a bit. Maybe I'll write more later. Or maybe I'll just sleep.

Friday, September 20

I actually managed to keep down a little bit of chicken at lunch today, so maybe I'm finally on the mend. I didn't feel like eating at dinner, but I'm not sick again, just not hungry. Jean-Mathias came by to see me after work today, to make sure I was doing okay. It was really sweet of him. I'm not sure what I did to deserve such a great friend, but I need to remember to tell him how much I appreciate him at some point. Probably not Sunday, given how bad I still feel, but maybe at lunch on Monday if I can go back to work then. I hope I can. Missing two days is bad enough. I don't want to make it more.

I think Mme Moreau made some incorrect assumptions about Jean-Mathias and our relationship. She didn't say anything exactly, but she had this sly smile on her face when she showed him upstairs.

I feel like I'm protesting too much when I tell people Jean-Mathias is my friend, nothing more, but it's the truth. We hang out and do stuff together, but he's never said or done anything to suggest he has more of an interest in me than friends. He knows I'm gay. Even if he wasn't interested, he would have told me if he shared my leanings. If not then, some other time. And if he isn't gay, then he can't be anything more than my friend. It doesn't work that way, even if I think it might be easier that way. Nothing with him is ever complicated, well, except our difference of opinion where Yves is concerned, but even that isn't complicated. We've agreed to disagree, and that's the end of it. We still do all the stuff we've always done together. We just don't talk about my love life like we did when I was dating (if you can call it that) Pierre.

Speaking of Pierre, he's been notably absent this month, except on Sundays when he still comes for dinner. He told his mother that with classes starting, he wouldn't have time to come home during the week. I truly hope that's the reason and not because he's uncomfortable with me being here. I'd hate to think I was keeping him from home, but I don't know how to ask without sounding egocentric at best and like a raving idiot at worst.

It's getting late. I should go to sleep so I can keep getting better.

Thursday, September 26

Yves finally called today. I was beginning to wonder if he'd forgotten about me or didn't want to see me anymore. He apologized for not calling sooner, saying he'd been so busy with the curators from Vienna that he hadn't had time for anything other than work. They left this afternoon, though, so Yves has some free time again. He suggested we make up for our cancelled plans last weekend by taking a trip together this weekend.

I told him I felt like that was rushing things a little, but I'd be happy to have dinner with him again or do something else here in Grenoble. He didn't sound too thrilled, but I have a feeling Yves wouldn't go for separate rooms like when I went to the vineyard with Pierre or separate beds like when Jean-Mathias and I went to Lyon. And I'm not ready for that. I wasn't ready for it with Pierre, and I'm not ready for it now. That doesn't mean I won't ever be, but I need more than a couple of dates first.

So we're going to dinner and then to the theater on Saturday night, which is good because I can still play football with Jean-Mathias on Sunday and won't have to feel bad about missing two weeks in a row.

Sunday, September 29

We went to the same restaurant last night as the last time Yves took me out, which is fine with me. I'm certainly not going to complain about an incredible meal. The play was an adaptation of <u>Caligula</u> by Jean-Paul Sartre, most of which went over my head, I'll admit. Existentialism is hard enough in English. It's pretty much beyond me in French, despite Madame Barbour's best attempts to pound it into my head in my twentieth century lit class. After it was over, Yves suggested we go back to his place for a nightcap. I wasn't entirely sure I should have said yes last night, and I'm still not sure I should have this morning, but I agreed anyway. I'm tired of feeling like a teenager, nervous and scared of anything approaching real life. That doesn't mean I'm going to run off with the first stranger I meet and offer him my virginity, but it does mean I'm at a point where I can make those choices for myself without needing anyone else's approval.

No, I didn't sleep with Yves. I'm not ready for that yet, but I did spend an awful lot of time kissing him on his couch last night. And an awful lot of time jerking off once I got home. I suspect he'd have done it for me if I'd given any indication I wanted it, but he didn't push, and I appreciate that. I suspect it won't be long before I'll give him anything he asks for.

I'm not sure if that's a good thing or a bad thing.

I'm going to call Alexandre this afternoon. I need to talk to someone before Yves and I have our date next weekend. He's making dinner for me at his apartment. I need to decide what I'm going to do before then, and I don't really want to bring it up with the whole group. I'm not quite comfortable with that level of sharing.

Tuesday, October 1

I'm meeting with Claude after work today. Alexandre is out of town for a few days, but Claude said he'd be glad to meet with me so we could talk. I'm not quite as comfortable with him as I am with Alexandre just because I don't know him as well, but he still has what I'm looking for in a relationship and in a spiritual life, so I hope he'll be able to help. I've got to decide what I'm going to do about Saturday, up to and including canceling the date if I decide I'm really that worried. I don't think I am. Yves didn't pressure me last weekend. I think it's more a question of deciding what my own limits are right now.

Claude was wonderful to talk to. I'm so glad I agreed, even if I thought I would've preferred talking to Alexandre. I told him the whole story, including the jerking off part. It was embarrassing, but he didn't make me feel that way. He told me that was perfectly normal and that I shouldn't be embarrassed by my physical urges. I didn't need to be ruled by them, but I didn't have to deny them either. We talked about dinner on Saturday, and he told me I had to trust my heart. If I felt like I was ready for more, if I felt like I could have the kind of relationship I want with Yves, then there was no harm in exploring a little more, but that if I wasn't sure, it was better to wait because any kind of physical component adds weight to a relationship. That isn't a bad thing, but it's something to be taken seriously, a decision to make with deliberation rather than with undue haste.

I'm not ready. I want to be. I want Yves to be the one for me, but I'm not at the point of committing to it yet, and until I am, we'll stay with kisses and I'll take care of myself when I get home. At least I can stop being uncomfortable on that score.

Thursday, October 3

It feels odd not having anything to write about David et Jonathan last night. It was good to be there as always, but since I didn't feel comfortable having the discussion with the whole group that I had with Claude alone on Tuesday, I didn't really feel like I had anything new to add, nor that I got anything huge out of the discussion. I guess that's normal. Not every meeting will be life-changing. That doesn't mean it wasn't worthwhile. Maybe something I said made a difference for someone else, and maybe it was simply part of the long-term growth that's as important as the huge breakthroughs.

Now if I can just get through this weekend, I'll be good.

Sunday, October 6

I really have to start writing more than twice a week, but I get busy or I feel like there's nothing new to add. So anyway, it's Sunday now. I worked the rest of the week, went to Pole Étudiant on Wednesday, had lunch with Jean-Mathias as usual, and then went to have dinner with Yves last night.

The food was delicious. I'm not sure why he always wants to eat out when he cooks as well as he does. We had dinner, shared a bottle of wine (or maybe a little more than that. I kind of lost track) and ended up back on his couch. I told him I wasn't ready to do more than just kiss, and he accepted that, although he did say it wouldn't always be enough. I know that, and I told him so, but I need a little more time.

He agreed, and he was as good as his word.

Mostly.

I mean, he didn't try to grope me or anything, but we did end up lying on the couch with him on top of me. There was something about having his weight on top of me. I don't even know if I can put it into words. I felt, I don't know, cornered but protected at the same time.

Like I couldn't go anywhere without his agreement but also like nothing could get at me without his permission. It was an odd mix of feelings, and I'm not entirely sure I like it. The protected bit, yes, but not the cornered part. Not in retrospect. Last night all I could do was pant into his kisses and try not to come in my pants from the friction of his body against my dick. He always stopped right about the point I thought I couldn't stop from coming, so I made it home with my dignity intact, but that's about all I can say for it.

Yves invited me to another museum function on Thursday. I told him I'd love to go with him, but that I'd have to come straight home afterward since I have to work on Friday. Once again he didn't seem thrilled with my insistence, but he agreed. He's obviously more comfortable and more casual about the physical side of a relationship than I am. He's had more time to get that way. I'm glad he seems willing to give me time to get comfortable because I want to reach a point where I don't think twice about being intimate with my lover.

I think the problem is that I'm not completely ready to think of him as my lover yet. The term boyfriend doesn't suit when he's in his late forties, but the term lover implies a degree of commitment we haven't made yet. Or maybe that's just me. Hell, that's probably just me.

I can't be anyone other than who I am, though, so we'll all have to live with it until I can get my shit together.

I'm hoping playing soccer will help today. It's been rainy all week and I haven't felt like swimming either, so I'm restless for that reason too. It's still cloudy today, but at least the rain has stopped. I think I'd go crazy cooped up inside for another day. I wonder what will happen when the snow starts falling, although I guess that's when skiing replaces football. Hmm… maybe I should look into a ski suit. Nothing I have for everyday wear would be warm enough. I'll have to find someone to give me lessons since I've never gone skiing, but it seems silly to spend a year at the foot of the Alps and not take advantage of it.

And once again I'm babbling. It's only October. I wonder when the ski season starts. No one has mentioned it yet, but maybe that's because it's obvious to them.

Sometimes I feel so out of my depth. And the solution to that is to ask the questions to get the answers I want. Yves said that's what drew his attention to me when we first met, the fact that I wasn't afraid to ask questions. So I'll ask this afternoon and see what the guys have to say.

Ski season in Courchevel starts at the beginning of December unless there isn't sufficient snowfall. The guys all wanted to know if I skied, and when I said I'd never been, they promised to teach me. Jean-Mathias even said he thought he had an old ski suit that might fit me. He said he'd call his mother and have her dig through his boxes of old clothes. He's a little taller than I am, so it makes sense he'd have one from a few years ago that might work for me.

So now I have to not make a fool of myself on the ski slopes since they were all talking about buying season passes. It's only an hour and a half to Courchevel from here so it's a day trip. Leave early in the morning on Saturday, ski until dark, have dinner there, and then drive home. Or drive down to Albertville for dinner (less expensive than Courchevel apparently) and then drive the rest of the way home after eating. Repeat on Sunday. And rent a chalet for the week between Christmas and New Year's. Of course they all own skis and boots and everything. I'll have to see how much renting them costs to decide if it's worth buying some and selling them used at the end of the season (which apparently goes through the end of April!). I freaked out a bit at hearing that, but they promised me it doesn't stay winter that long in Grenoble, just up in the mountains. Thank goodness. I don't think I could handle six months of snow.

I also talked with Pierre a little after dinner, trying to make sure there weren't any hard feelings between us. He assured me he barely had time to eat during the week, much less come all the way across town to his parents' house to eat. I didn't think the university was that far away, but it is on the other side of the pedestrian zone, which means taking an indirect route since you can't drive through centre ville. Still, he seemed sincere, so I'll take him at his word and stop feeling guilty about it.

Thursday, October 10

I'm at home now, waiting for Yves to pick me up for the reception. I don't remember what this one is for. If he told me, I was too high on his kisses to remember. I don't imagine that will be much of a problem tonight since we'll be at a public reception. I can't decide if that's good or bad. I mean, I'm glad he wants me to go with him to events and things, that I'm not some dirty little secret, but the evening at his apartment was so intimate, not just because of the kissing but because we could spend the evening focused entirely on each other. There's definitely something seductive about being the center of Yves's attention. He's so vibrant, so potent, that when he stares at me, my insides turn to mush and I just want to surrender to whatever he wants. So far I think I've resisted acting like a maiden in distress even if he kind of makes me feel like the heroine in some trashy romance novel, all weak in the knees because the hero is so much of a man. Not that I'd know from reading them, but Teresa used to complain about how the women in her books would always react to the, how did she put it? potent masculinity of the hero. We laughed about it because, come on, guys like that don't exist in real life.

The egg's on my face right about now because that's exactly how Yves makes me feel. Somehow I doubt Teresa would appreciate the observation now any more than she appreciated the books then. She doesn't mind that I'm gay (she's actually the first person I told), but she'd smack me for being stupid about it.

Except it doesn't feel stupid. It feels good. Like I don't have to be completely in control of everything. I can relax and let Yves take care of details. I can relax and let him guide me through the physical side of our relationship. That doesn't make me girly or weak. It makes me young and inexperienced, and those are facts I can't (or won't) change in a hurry. Fortunately neither seems to be a problem for Yves, so I'm going to stop obsessing about it. It's time for me to go downstairs to wait for him anyway.

I'm home. The reception only lasted until ten, but I still insisted Yves bring me home afterward. If we'd gone to his apartment, who knows how late we'd have stayed there, and I have to work tomorrow. I wish the reception had been tomorrow so we could have spent more time together. He told me he's leaving on Saturday for three weeks, a reverse visit to the one last week with the Viennese curators. He's going to Vienna to supervise the packing and moving of the exhibit that's coming here and won't be back until November. I'm not sure why he's leaving on Saturday instead of Monday, but that's his business, not mine.

I'll miss him. I don't see him or even talk to him every day, but I've gotten used to anticipating seeing him. I guess I'll anticipate seeing him in November now. He did promise to call often so I didn't forget him (his words) while he was gone. That's kind of sweet, actually.

So I guess it's back to my normal routine. Work, lunch with Jean-Mathias, Pole Étudiant on Wednesdays and football on Sundays, weather permitting. I wonder what they do in November when it'll be too cold for football but not ski season yet. I should suggest we find an indoor basketball court. Then we'd be playing a game I'm actually good at for once. I can swim for the exercise, of course, but I'd miss the camaraderie if we went for a month without getting together.

Thursday, October 24

I can't believe it's been two weeks since I've picked up my journal. Sure, I've missed a day or two (or four) before now, but I've never gone this long. I've got to do better about that. The thing is, nothing particularly interesting happened. I worked, I ate lunch with Jean-Mathias, I played basketball with the guys since it's rained the past two Sundays and they knew where to find an indoor basketball court. Nothing exciting. I'm looking forward to this weekend, though. Romain suggested we go to Aix-en-Provence this weekend. Apparently they're filming some big-budget action film there and he wants to see if we can catch glimpses of any of the actors. Actually I think he wants to see if we can catch a glimpse of Angelina Jolie, who's in the film, but I'll settle for catching a glimpse of Tom Hardy. And I haven't been to Aix-en-Provence, so if I get bored actor stalking, I'll wander the city instead. I've read up on it a bit so I'll know what my options are. It's called the City of Fountains, but I don't know how many of them will be running in October. We'll just have to see.

I'm not sure who's going exactly, besides Jean-Mathias and Romain. Romain said he'd borrow his mother's van if enough people want to go, so I'm not particularly worried about it. We're meeting at his house after work tomorrow to drive the three hours to Aix, so I'll find out then.

I haven't told Yves about going with the guys. I don't know how he'd react. I mean, it's just a weekend with friends, but he comes across as possessive sometimes. I'm not going to give up my friends, even for him, but he's not in town to argue with me over it. There's no harm in going with them. If it's a problem, we can argue about it when we get back.

He has called every couple of days, which is nice. He says he misses me, that Vienna isn't nearly as interesting by himself and he wishes I was there with him so he could show me around and show me off. It's nice to be missed and to know that he wants to introduce me to people. It makes me feel proud, which is ridiculous in a way. I don't need his approval to feel good about myself, but at the same time, it's nice to be with someone who appreciates me and wants to be seen with me. I wouldn't want to be someone's secret.

I need to pack for the weekend and then go to bed so I'm up on time for work.

Sunday, October 27

We had a great time in Aix-en-Provence. I did get a glimpse of Tom Hardy, and Romain actually got Angelina Jolie's autograph, which was cool. He wanted to keep hanging around the set, but Jean-Mathias and Xavier got bored with that (so did I) so we visited the city some instead. It was a Roman city, so the baths are still there and stuff like that. Very interesting. A lot more preserved that what Jean-Mathias and I saw in Lyon. Most of that was just foundations or archeological digs. Here, it was full buildings still. Xavier said if I really want to see Roman stuff, I should go to Arles or Nîmes. I also want to get up to the more northern parts of France, but there's no rush. I've still got months here, and some vacation time coming eventually.

In other news, Yves gets back on Friday. We haven't made plans for the weekend although I hope I'll get to see him, but I know traveling can be tiring and I don't know what he'll have to do at the museum as far as intake of the exhibit. If not this weekend, maybe early next week. As long as it's not Wednesday, I'm free.

I haven't really written a lot about it because I'm not entirely comfortable writing about it, but I've jerked off every time we've talked. Not while we were talking, but afterward. I'm ready to lift my kissing-only ban. I'm so tired of my own hand. I'm not ready for anal sex yet (I'm squirming just writing it), but I am ready for more. I haven't told Yves that, but I will the next time we're alone together.

I just hope that's soon.

Thursday, October 31

Yves is home. He called to say he'd made it to his apartment and would I like to spend the day together on Saturday. He didn't specify doing what and I didn't ask. It doesn't matter. I just want to see him and hear more about Vienna and the exhibit and everything. I'm going over to his apartment around ten on Saturday and we'll decide what to do from there.

Jean-Mathias scowled at me when I told him I didn't know if I'd be at basketball on Sunday since Yves was back in town, but I reminded him that I'm allowed to have a life too. He couldn't exactly argue with that. It's not like he's my boyfriend. Yves is, and I haven't seen him in three weeks.

Friday, November 1

La Toussaint.

All Saints Day, the day to remember all those who have gone before us.

I walked through the cimitière Saint Roch today at the suggestion of Père Bernard, the priest at St. Louis. The graves were covered in chrysanthemums, the flower of death here, because it's traditional for people to visit the graves of their family members. As I looked around, I saw, in some cases, generations of the same family all buried in one section of the cemetery. It was really stunning. I know on a conscious level that history is longer here and that roots go deeper, but this really drove it home. My family's been in Texas for three generations. There are families who have been in Grenoble since it was founded in the 11th century. That's a heck of a lot more than a hundred years.

We didn't have to work because of La Toussaint. Everyone goes with their families, some of whom are elsewhere in the country. I can't remember the last time I went to my great-grandmother's grave. I know where it is, but it isn't something I think about doing. I'll have to remember this next year when All Saints Day rolls around and go visit her and all my other relatives.

Saturday, November 2

I'm sitting here staring into space with a silly grin on my face. I can see my reflection in the window and I look like a complete goofball, but I can't stop smiling. Life is good.

Today was fantastic. I took the bus over to Yves's apartment this morning and we spent the entire day together. He hadn't eaten breakfast yet so we went to a little café near his house for coffee and pastries. He held my hand the entire time, which sounds simple, but we were out in public and I'm not used to that. After we'd eaten, we went back to Yves's apartment and spent pretty much the rest of the afternoon on his couch. We talked about what we'd done while he was gone. He told me all about Vienna, repeating several times how much he'd missed me. I told him about Aix-en-Provence. He wasn't particularly happy about it, but he didn't make a big deal about it either. He wants to be the one taking me places and showing me things. So I suggested we plan a trip together. He said next weekend was too soon to plan something really nice, so we're going in two weeks. He said he'd make all the arrangements and surprise me if I was okay with that. I agreed as long as he let me pay him back for my half. He didn't seem happy about that either, but he eventually agreed. I have a feeling I'm going to have to ask to see receipts if I really want to pay half, but maybe it's not worth arguing over. My mother always told me that the biggest part of staying married was deciding not to argue over stupid things. This probably qualifies as one of those things. Yves makes a whole lot more money than I do, to judge by his standard of living, so it's not like he's hurting his budget to pay for things for me. And I'm not taking it for granted that he'll pay for me so I'm not freeloading when he does. I need to stop stressing about this so much.

The trip isn't what has the silly grin on my face, as much as I'm looking forward to it.

Obviously we'd kissed off and on the entire time we were talking, but after we'd decided on the trip, things got a little more intense. I ended up lying underneath Yves on the couch again (that feeling is getting addictive) and I told him he didn't have to stop at kissing me.

I kind of expected him to go straight for my pants. I'm not sure why, but that's what I had in my head. I guess because when I jerk off, that's what I do. He didn't do that. He lingered. He touched me all over, all the while kissing me with those amazing kisses. By the time he finally undid my pants, I felt like I was going to explode. And then he touched me and I did.

I returned the favor because it felt wrong not to. I mean, if I'm okay with him doing something to me, I should be okay with doing it to him. It felt awkward, though, maybe because the angle was different. All in all, not the same feeling of euphoria from having him touch me. I'm not entirely sure what that's all about. Maybe I should call Claude again. I need to talk to someone, but this wouldn't be a question for Jean-Mathias even if he didn't mind me talking about Yves. I'm not entirely sure I can ask Claude. Not that I think he'd be offended. I'm not sure I can make myself talk about it out loud. I don't think of myself as being a prude, but we didn't talk about stuff like that at home or in college.

The problem is not knowing if what I'm doing is right. I know sex isn't wrong, but for me it belongs in the context of marriage. That would be great if I were straight and could easily define when I was married and when I wasn't, but I can't get married in Texas right now, and who knows if I'll ever be able to. So if I don't have a wedding to give me that marker, then I have to figure out some other way to define when it's acceptable and when it isn't. And then, of course, there's the question of what constitutes sex. Anything that elicits an orgasm (in which case I was damned before I started anything with Yves for jerking off)? Anything involving penetration? Where's the line? I don't have the answers, and that makes me feel uncertain, guilty even, for doing something I'm not sure I should be doing.

So I guess the first question is what constitutes to me the equivalent of being married. A commitment, I think. It doesn't have to be a formal commitment ceremony like I know some gay couples have. Marriage is a public proclamation of an internal commitment. If my boyfriend and I make that internal commitment, then we're as good as married, at least until we live somewhere that lets us get married legally.

That's the easy part, I guess, and it's also easy to say I'm not at that point yet with Yves. I think I could get to that point, but not yet.

The hard part is where along the continuum of sexual acts does one cross from messing around to getting serious.

Tonight felt pretty damn serious.

I wasn't completely naked, but almost. All the important parts were bare. He had my shirt open and my pants undone and pushed down. I came all over his hand and then he did the same on mine. It felt a lot bigger, more important than just jacking off. Probably because it wasn't just me. So did we have sex? And if we did, have I sinned?

I wish I knew the answers. Life would be so much easier if I did.

I need to get over myself. A man like Yves isn't going to have patience with my hang-ups for long.

Wednesday, November 6

I called Claude back earlier this week, and both he and Alexandre were free to meet before David et Jonathan tonight so I met them early for coffee. I'm not sure I can remember a more awkward conversation as I tried to tell them what had happened with Yves and explain my feelings about it in a language that still sometimes eludes me. They were very patient with me and a little concerned Yves was pressuring me into something I'm not ready for. I assured them Yves hadn't pressured me at all. If anyone was pressuring anyone, it was me pressuring myself as I fought with my doubts and my guilt and not wanting to lose Yves, but not wanting to compromise my beliefs either.

I didn't tell them about the trip next weekend. I have a feeling they wouldn't approve. They didn't say that outright, but I could tell they were worried for me. I appreciate the sentiment, but I'm not being pressured into something I'm not comfortable with.

If Yves only wanted sex, he wouldn't bother taking me out or having evenings like the one on Sunday where we kissed hello and goodbye but really nothing more than that. Sure, they were the same toe-curling kisses as always, but if he were intent on pressuring me into having sex with him, he wouldn't have stopped there. He would have taken me back to his place and tried to talk me into a repeat of Saturday or more. And he didn't do that. I can't figure out why everyone is so convinced he's out to take advantage of me.

It's a little frustrating feeling like nobody's on my side in this. I want to share what's going on in my life with my friends, but I shouldn't have to defend myself. I'm not doing anything wrong and neither is Yves. We haven't talked about the future yet, but there's time for that. And right now, he's treating me really well. He takes me out, he includes me in things related to his work. And when he kisses me, the world disappears. What is there to justify or defend about that? We have a good time together and he makes me feel good.

Maybe writing in this stupid journal wasn't such a good idea after all, if all it's going to do is make me angrier.

Sunday, November 17

I'm home from my trip with Yves. I haven't been writing because I haven't wanted to get into all that frustration and anger and defensiveness, but I had to write about the trip. Yves took me back to

Paris for the weekend. We left Friday afternoon, took the TGV (first class!), and stayed in the heart of the Marais at this posh hotel. Everything was first class all the way, from the train to the hotel to the restaurants and the seats at the theater. Talk about wining and dining! We shared a hotel room and a bed, which was its own intimacy. He didn't press for anything else, although we did spend a fair amount of time repeating past intimacies.

It's amazing what a little perspective can do. What felt odd two weeks ago doesn't feel nearly as odd after spending half the weekend touching Yves. He's always so tender with me afterward (not that he isn't tender other times too), getting a wash cloth to clean us up, stroking my hair, that sort of thing.

It's enough to convince me everyone else has no idea what they're talking about.

We didn't do a lot of touristy stuff on this trip, more cultural stuff. He did take me to the Louvre, but other than that, it was nice restaurants, a bit of shopping, and a play on Saturday night.

I missed church today. Yves had planned a special brunch for us, not realizing I would want to go to church, and I didn't feel right messing up his plans. And I couldn't go this evening because we didn't get home in time. I'll get online and find a daily Mass somewhere in town and go tomorrow evening. It's not quite the same, but at least I won't have skipped a week entirely.

Is it too soon to decide I'm in love? I feel like I'm floating after the weekend. Yves is perfect, almost too good to be true. He's considerate of me in public, opening doors for me, keeping me close when we're out, making me feel like he's proud to be seen with me, and when we're in private, he makes it clear he's interested in me without making me feel like we have to go to bed right away or making me feel like we have to do more than I'm comfortable with. Life with him would be full of receptions and cultural events and parties, of travel and high society.

I'm hesitant to bring up church, although it hasn't really been a problem up until now. We aren't usually together on Sunday mornings, except this weekend, and he's never asked me out for a Wednesday night so that hasn't been a problem either. If we plan another trip, I can always tell him then that I'd like to be able to go to church, either Saturday evening, Sunday morning, or Sunday evening. Time is flexible. There are churches with Masses at different times all over the city, and I'm sure that's true in any sizeable city. If we went to Courchevel, maybe not, but Yves hasn't shown any interest in any kind of sports, so I doubt he'd be proposing a weekend at a ski resort. And if I'm wrong, I'll deal with it then.

For now, I have to figure out what I'm going to say when Jean-Mathias asks about my weekend so I don't lie to him or argue with him over it. I hate the idea of having to choose between his friendship and seeing Yves. I really hope he'll reach a point where he can be happy for me.

Monday, November 18

Jean-Mathias is leaving for Africa for his sister's wedding in about two weeks. I'd forgotten about that. I mean, he told me, but it hasn't really come up again since he didn't take his full vacation in August. He's taking those extra weeks starting December 1. He'll be back at the beginning of January.

I need to remember to tell Yves I won't be free on Sunday the next two weekends. If Jean-Mathias is going to be gone, I want to spend as much time with him as I can. I don't think I'd realized how much I depend on his smile to get me through the day when an experiment goes wrong or the data are inconclusive or the opposite of what I expected. We may not agree on the subject of Yves, but he really has been an extraordinary friend to me. Almost everyone I socialize with is someone I've met through him. I mean, there's Claude and Alexandre from David et Jonathan and my friends at the Pole

Étudiant, but while I look forward to seeing them, Xavier and Romain and the other guys from football and now basketball are the ones I hang out with on the weekends, the ones I travel with (besides Yves).

I should call Yves now.

That didn't go the way I'd hoped. I mean, it's not like we made plans and I canceled them. I simply called to tell him I had made plans. He didn't quite go ballistic, but he wasn't happy. He actually asked me if I was sleeping around behind his back. I promised him I wasn't because I wouldn't do that. I don't know if he believed me. I offered to spend Friday evening and all day Saturday with him both weekends so he'd know I wasn't picking Jean-Mathias over him. Of course if I tell Jean-Mathias that, he'll say Yves shouldn't make me choose. He's right, but it isn't a question of choosing. I can be friends with Jean-Mathias and go out with Yves. They don't have to be mutually exclusive.

I'm so tired of this back and forth pull. When did my life get so complicated?

Saturday, November 23

I spent last night at Yves's apartment. I think he'd have liked me to stay again tonight, but I needed to come home and think.

He was different last night and today. I'm not really sure how to explain it. More possessive than usual, more demanding of my attention. He's always been comfortable holding my hand if we were out, that sort of thing, but last night it felt like he was almost groping me, sliding his hand up my thigh under the table, putting his arm around my waist with his hand almost on my ass instead of around my side. Like he was trying to stake a claim or something.

It made me a little uncomfortable, honestly, but he told me to stop being silly when I mentioned it after we got home. I guess it was silly. It's not like he stuck his hand down my pants or anything, and nobody seemed at all bothered by us so it obviously wasn't as big a deal as I felt like it was.

When we finally went to bed, Yves was all over me even more than usual, not just his hands this time but his mouth as well.

I thought he made me feel good with his hands on me, but feeling him take me in his mouth… words fail me.

I didn't offer to reciprocate. I know I'm not ready for that, and he didn't force the issue, thank goodness.

He apologized this morning for being angry with me last night and suggested we do something fun today. Our definitions of fun aren't exactly the same. He listed all the other museums in Grenoble to visit. I suggested swimming or basketball. We settled on a drive through the wine country southwest of here. He took me to a couple of his favorite wineries where they actually know him by name. High society indeed.

We actually ate dinner at one of the wineries before we came back. He asked if I'd stay again tonight, but I asked him to bring me home and he did. So now I have to figure out what I feel about last night.

The argument itself, the cause of it, and the blow job afterward.

I just wish I knew what had caused his odd behavior in the first place. If I knew that, maybe I'd know if my unease was justified.

As for the blow job, I can't even begin to describe how good it felt in the moment, but afterward it left me uneasy, like we'd gone too far without settling things between us, from the fight and more generally. I still haven't asked him what he hopes for where we're concerned. I haven't asked him about church. There's so much we need to discuss, but it never seems to be the right time to bring it up.

I guess I need to make it the right time. I'm seeing him again on Tuesday. He offered to make dinner so we'd have some privacy without it getting too late on a work night. I'll bring it up then.

Tuesday, November 26

So much for bringing anything up. By the time I got to Yves's apartment (I had an experiment at work that I miscalculated so I didn't get to leave on time), he had dinner ready. I didn't want to spoil the lovely meal with serious conversation, and after dinner, we ended up in bed practically before I could swallow the last bit of my coffee. It was even more intense than Friday. After he'd sucked my brains out through my dick (yes, I know that's crude, but it's the way I felt), he climbed on top of me, obviously wanting me to return the favor.

I couldn't do it. I tried, but it freaked me out too much. Fortunately he let it go and let me jerk him off. I thought about trying to talk to him as he drove me home, but that's hardly the right venue for a serious conversation. I'm going to see him again on Saturday evening. He has a commitment at work on Friday night that's staff only. I'll miss seeing him, of course, but I can hardly complain about his work.

I really do have to talk to him then, though. Yes, he backed off tonight when I couldn't make myself do what he asked, but I felt bad about it, and that's not good. That means I'm feeling pressured, and I don't want that. If he really is pressuring me, then maybe everyone's right after all. I don't want to think that. I want what we had in Paris, or actually any time before last Friday.

It's not that I'm opposed to the sex or even opposed to giving him a blow job eventually. I just need to know this is real, that he's as committed to making this work as I am. I know that sounds kind of silly given that I'm going home in June, but June is a long time from now, and if I really have a reason to stay, well…

I shouldn't let myself think that way. Not until we've had a chance to talk about what we want out of our relationship.

Saturday, November 30

I broke up with Yves tonight.

Just writing the words makes my heart hurt and my stomach tie in knots and I can't do this tonight. I'll simply say thank you, Jesus, for Jean-Mathias and try to write the rest tomorrow when, hopefully, it won't hurt to breathe anymore.

Monday, December 2

I couldn't write yesterday either. I made myself go to work today. Jean-Mathias wasn't there, which was almost too much. I did manage to go to church last night, finally. I couldn't go in the morning. I wasn't even at a point where I could pray, and that is a terribly frightening feeling for someone who has always depended on prayer as a source of solace.

I'm still not entirely sure I'm up to writing this, but I know it will help me feel better. At least I'll stop dreading the telling of it once it's down, even if it doesn't help.

The short version is that Yves is a cheating bastard who wanted two things from me: a pretty boy on his arm in public and a twink in his bed. I'm not willing to be either of those things, not without more of a commitment than he was apparently willing to make.

The evening started out well enough. I went there around six as we'd agreed and got there about the same time he did, his arms full of purchases for dinner. I sat with him in the kitchen while he fixed our food. I tried to bring up my concerns, but he said we shouldn't spoil a lovely meal with such serious talk and we could talk after we ate.

When we finished eating, we went into the living room to talk, Yves said, but he didn't give me a chance, pulling me into his arms and kissing me. I'm not a saint. I'm not proof against him when he touches me like that. He got me mostly undressed and all worked up, and then he pulled open his pants and said he'd been waiting since last Friday to feel my mouth on him. I told him again I wasn't ready. He laughed at me and asked me what I took him for.

I told him I took him for my lover, but that I needed him to be patient with me, that I'd never done this before and I needed more time.

That went over like a lead balloon.

He scoffed at the idea that I was twenty-two and hadn't ever done this before. And if I'd done it before, I could damn well do it to him.

I tried to explain about my upbringing and college and my beliefs. That only made it worse. By the time he was done ridiculing everything that's important to me, I was nearly in tears. I stumbled to my feet and got dressed. Fortunately I grabbed my jacket on the way out because my wallet and phone were in it, but of course the buses weren't running anymore.

I didn't know what else to do so I called Jean-Mathias. I guess I could have called Mme Moreau, but that would have been complicated. Jean-Mathias told me to start walking toward the river so I'd be away from Yves's house in case he decided to come after me. Not sure why he thought Yves would do that when he was obviously done with me, but I did as he said. He met me at the river less than ten minutes later. It all came spilling out. He didn't judge me. He just held my hand and let me rage. He didn't even say I told you so.

It was already late and he had to finish packing on Sunday, so he took me home after that, but he made me promise to wait for him. He said, "Don't find someone else while I'm gone."

I didn't know whether to laugh or cry when he said it. I think I did a little of both. God knows my attempts at finding someone else the last time he was gone ended in disaster. Besides, after having everything I am and believe in thrown in my face, I'm pretty sure it will take me some time to be ready for another relationship.

I have to believe the person God intended for me is out there somewhere. I just have to find him. I tried too hard with Yves, I guess, wanting him to be something he wasn't.

He said he'd slept with a "boy like me" in Vienna because I wasn't putting out and he could only be expected to go so long without getting some.

It makes me wonder now about those nights he had to work late or attend a staff-only function. Was he really at work or was he with some random hook-up getting what I wouldn't give him?

The sad part is that I would have given him anything he wanted, in time, if he'd been the man I thought he was.

I didn't play basketball with the guys yesterday, but I do have Romain's number so if I'm feeling like company by the end of the week, I'll see if they're planning on skiing and if I can tag along. Jean-Mathias found a ski suit for me a couple of weeks ago so I have that if I'm up to it. And if not next weekend, there will be other chances. Right now I'm still licking my wounds, and the last thing I want is the guys asking me what's wrong. I'd make a fool of myself trying to tell them.

Friday, December 6

I called Romain tonight. I'm going skiing with them tomorrow. I can't keep sitting around the house moping. I didn't even make it to David et Jonathan on Wednesday. Claude called to check on me, so I told him a little of what happened. He made me promise to call him when I was ready to talk. I guess I'll be ready to talk at some point. At least if we're skiing, there won't be much chance for talking about anything other than how idiotic I look on skis since I have no idea what I'm doing. The rest of the guys didn't know about Yves, so I don't have to worry about them asking me about him.

They might notice I'm not my usual cheerful self, but I'll worry about that if they say anything. I can always tell them something happened at work.

Saturday, December 7

Skiing was a lot of fun, a lot of exercise, but a lot of fun. I'm glad I went. It helped being outside in the sun today. They're going again tomorrow. I passed. I'm going to church and then I'm going to call Claude and Alexandre. I don't know if they'll be free tomorrow on such short notice, but I'm ready to talk to someone. I don't know what they'll have to say, but I'm ready to listen.

Sunday, December 8

Claude and Alexandre were free this afternoon, much to my relief. We talked for a long, long time about Yves and what I wanted and what went wrong. I told them all of it, and they told me I did the right thing. I don't think I realized how much I needed to hear that. Jean-Mathias promised me everything would be all right. He listened to me and let me cry and didn't say I told you so, but that isn't the same as hearing flat out that I did the right thing.

They told me I don't have to accept being treated in a way I wouldn't treat others, that I don't have to accept being cheated on or ridiculed or pressured into anything. We prayed together for comfort and wisdom and the strength to continue my search for the person I was meant to be with.

I left their house today with such a sense of peace. Yes, it still hurts. It may always hurt to think of Yves and the mistakes I made with him, but at least I got out when I did, before he talked me into something I would truly have regretted instead of only into something I'll learn from, but with no lasting harm.

He would have wanted to fuck me, to put it crudely, and eventually I would have let him. If he'd been genuine in his caring for me, if he'd been willing to commit to me and respect me and love me, that would be fine. Sex is a part of a healthy adult relationship, but he didn't want those things. He wanted arm candy, a pretty boy to show off at museum functions and fuck in the evenings. I need more than that out of a relationship. I'm better off without him.

I can write those words, but I wonder how long it will be before I truly believe them.

I guess only time will tell.

Saturday, December 14

Another week gone. Only two more weeks until Jean-Mathias comes home. I can't believe how much I miss him. I don't think I realized how much he'd become part of my life. He's been my support from the moment we met. I wouldn't have friends if it weren't for him. I wouldn't be busy every weekend I want to be. I wouldn't have learned how to ski. I'd eat alone at lunch every day. I'd pretty much be a hermit if it weren't for him. I'm not now, even with him gone, because he's as generous with his friends as he is with his spirit. It never occurred to him not to include me in things he does because he doesn't need to keep me to himself or his friends to himself. He knows one doesn't take away from the other.

I keep catching myself looking for him at odd moments, turning to share this thought or that with him, but of course he isn't there.

Oh, fuck.

Oh, fuck, fuck, fuck, fuck.

I'm as blind as I am stupid.

When did I fall in love with Jean-Mathias?

I just reread my journal from the beginning because this doesn't seem like a realization I should only be having now, five and a half months after meeting him. And the answer is probably within a few days of meeting him, except he's straight and Pierre wasn't, so it was easier to go out with Pierre than pine over Jean-Mathias. And then after Pierre and I broke up, Yves swept me off my feet before I could blink and I didn't have to think about it. The reality, though, is that once Jean-Mathias and I met, there are all of maybe three entries where he isn't mentioned at least in passing. Even in the midst of breaking up with Yves, there he was, taking care of me.

Of course, there's still the problem that he's straight because even if he isn't interested in me, surely he would have told me he was gay at some point in the past five months, or his friends would have mentioned an ex-boyfriend or something. Unless he isn't out yet, but that's almost as bad as being straight. I mean, I'm not going to tell anyone if he doesn't want me to (assuming he's in the closet and not straight, of course) but I can't have the relationship I want with someone who can't admit to who he is and what we have. So straight or in the closet, it's still pointless to be in love with him.

Except he made me promise to wait for him. "Don't fall for someone else while I'm gone."

When he first said it and in my grief over everything that happened with Yves, I chalked it up to having met Yves while Jean-Mathias was gone last time and him wanting to meet anyone else I got together with before things had a chance to get serious this time. Now I can't help but wonder and maybe even hope a little that he meant it another way, that he wants to be with me as a boyfriend rather than just a friend.

Of course there's no way of knowing any of that until he gets home, and even then I haven't the slightest idea how to bring it up without making things really, really awkward if I'm wrong and he really did just mean my abysmal luck with Yves.

I suppose this could be another question for Claude and Alexandre, and maybe I could sound out Romain or Xavier a bit on the subject of Jean-Mathias's exes. That would be tacky, though, wouldn't it?

It probably would be, but if I can find out for sure that he's only dated girls in the past, I'll know to keep my mouth shut. That's got to be better than making a fool of myself and losing a friend in the process. And if he has dated guys, then I can hope he could feel about me the way I feel about him. Maybe not already, but someday. Enough to want to give it a try.

Because I know one thing beyond a shadow of a doubt: Jean-Mathias would never treat me the way Yves did. I'm not saying we wouldn't disagree. We've already disagreed where Yves was concerned, and while that wasn't exactly a happy occasion, it didn't keep us from staying friends. And yes, it's easier to be friends than to be lovers, but we have such a base of common interests and activities that it could be exactly what I'm looking for if he's interested.

He even shares my faith enough to be a part of that spiritual journey. Again, we don't agree on everything and maybe it doesn't have the same place in his life as it has in mine, but it does have a place in his life, which is more than I could say for Pierre or Yves, and that's already a huge improvement.

I guess I have to wait for January to get here so I can see what happens next. I have a feeling this is going to be the longest three weeks of my life.

Saturday, December 28

Jean-Mathias is supposed to get back today, although the lab is closed until January 6 because of New Year's and everyone going on vacation. Would it seem too eager to call him tomorrow?

It probably would. He'll be jetlagged and exhausted from the trip and that would just be rude.

I've met with Claude and Alexandre several more times since I realized I'm in love with Jean-Mathias. They cautioned me about rushing into anything, about rebound relationships and everything else. I know they're right and heaven knows my track record has been abysmal up until now, but that's the beauty of it. I already know Jean-Mathias is different. I've worked with him, joked with him, eaten lunch with him, traveled with him, played football and basketball with him. The only thing I haven't done with him is kiss him or tell him how I feel about him.

I'm not going to rush into doing those things. I didn't have any luck finding out anything about Jean-Mathias's exes. My tentative questions were met with a universal reply: ask Jean-Mathias. It's good to know his friends are discreet, but it's kind of frustrating at the same time.

Phone's ringing.

I guess it wouldn't have been rude to call tomorrow since that was Jean-Mathias calling me. He landed in Paris and is waiting to get his bags to take the train home. He wanted to know if I wanted to come over tomorrow night. He said he'd worried about me a lot while he was gone and he wanted to make sure I was okay.

Now that he's home and I'm going to get to see him again, I'm just fine. I'll have to be careful what I say and do. The last time he saw me, I was so upset over Yves that I could barely form a coherent sentence. I have a lot to share with him before I can even think about saying anything about the way I feel, if I ever can, but at least I'll be able to see him. At least I'll know he's only a phone call away if I need him because even as distraught as I was when Yves and I broke up, I knew he'd come if I called.

The guys were talking about going skiing again tomorrow, but I think I'll skip it. I didn't buy a Christmas present for Jean-Mathias, but I'd really like to give him one so I'll go shopping tomorrow and see what I can find. I have no idea what I'll get him, but I'll know it when I see it.

I wonder if I'll sleep tonight. It seems like I've had a lot of sleepless nights over the past month, between not sleeping because I was grieving over Yves and not sleeping because I couldn't stop thinking about Jean-Mathias.

Now that he's home, maybe I'll be able to rest again, at least after we've had a chance to talk some.

Sunday, December 29

I found the perfect gift for Jean-Mathias today, or at least it seems perfect to me. It's a print of two old men sitting side by side staring at the ocean. You can just tell from looking at it that they're best friends and that they've been coming to that spot and sitting there together for more years than either of them cares to count. Friends or lovers, I hope Jean-Mathias and I are those two men, still sitting together and sharing things when we're ninety.

The next stop is mine. Better put this away.

Monday, December 30

I am never, ever getting drunk again. It's Monday morning, and my head is pounding. I feel like I'm going to puke. And I babbled to Jean-Mathias last night. I didn't quite come out and tell him I'd fallen in love with him, but almost. The evening started really well, with me giving him the picture and him giving me a figurine he'd brought back from Africa that's supposed to bring blessings to your marriage. He said he hoped I'd appreciate it for the moment when I finally found the person I was searching for.

I almost said something right then, but I didn't want to rush, so I just said thank you. He opened a bottle of wine and we started talking and drinking. The next thing I knew, it was several hours later, we'd barely stopped talking or drinking, and there were three empty wine bottles on the table. We talked about Africa, about his sister's wedding, about everything except Yves. I told him about meeting with Alexandre and Claude, about skiing with the guys, about everything I did while he was gone, just not about how I felt about all of it.

He turned to me seriously, hand on my shoulder, and asked me if I was doing okay. And that's when it slipped out. That the picture wasn't just about being friends, that I was interested in him.

He patted me on the head, kissed my cheek, and told me it was time for me to get some rest, that we'd talk in the morning when I was sober. I can't decide if that means he isn't interested or that he didn't believe me or what that means. I wonder if I can sneak out without waking him up. I can't face him. He's got to think I'm the most pathetic creature on the face of the earth right about now.

He's calling, telling me he has coffee. So much for sneaking out. I guess I'd better go face the music and hope I haven't lost my best friend.

Maybe things aren't as hopeless as I thought they were.

I'm not even sure where to begin. At the beginning, I guess.

I went out and took the coffee Jean-Mathias gave me, not really able to meet his eyes. He let me get away with that for a while. When I finished the first cup and was ready to stop hiding, I looked up. He handed me a towel and a change of clothes and said I'd feel better after a shower.

So I used his bathroom and cleaned up, and he was right. I did feel a little better.

When I came back out, he was on the couch watching TV. He switched it off and told me to come sit beside him, so I did. He asked me how much I remembered of last night. I wanted the cushions to swallow me up, but of course they didn't, so I had to tell him I remembered everything. I was drunk enough to lose my inhibitions, not my memories.

He said that was good and leaned over and kissed me.

I couldn't help it. I kissed him back, and it felt more right than anything in my life.

When we finally broke apart, I had to ask him why he hadn't said anything before now, and he said it was because I'd always been with someone else. He didn't know I was gay until I was already with Pierre, and when he came back from vacation, I'd already met Yves. He refused to be responsible for breaking up a relationship, so as long as I was with someone else, he was content to stay my friend. He wasn't going to say anything now either because I was just over a relationship, but then I was so much happier than when he last saw me that he started to hope maybe it was possible after all. And then to his surprise, I approached him last night. He didn't answer me then because he was afraid it was the wine talking, not my heart, and that I didn't know what I was saying or that I'd regret saying it in the morning.

The only thing I regret is being blind for so long.

We talked for a long time after that, about what went wrong with Yves, about our expectations for a relationship, about our experience (or lack of experience in my case), about work and the guys and what all of this means.

It's so refreshing to have that out of the way first instead of having it hanging over everything like a dark cloud of uncertainty. I'm sure we'll have more things to discuss as we move forward, but we're starting on the same page, and that's precious beyond words.

We spent all day together. Eventually we got hungry and went to get something to eat, and it was just as comfortable as it's always been. We ran into Romain while we were out. I thought they were going skiing today, but he has a cold and decided spending the day on the slopes might not be a good idea. He joined us for lunch, and it was as relaxed as always. At one point, Jean-Mathias reached over and squeezed my hand while we were talking. Romain blinked a couple of times, looked back and forth between the two of us, and muttered, "About time." And that was the entirety of the discussion.

I asked Jean-Mathias about it when we got home, but he swore he hadn't said anything to Romain about his feelings for me, that Romain must have picked up on everything we missed in each other. I guess that makes sense. I mean, when I went back and reread my journal, it seemed obvious in hindsight, just not at the time. An outsider probably would have seen it long before we did, or before I did anyway, since Jean-Mathias knew what he was feeling but chose not to act on it out of respect for my previous relationships.

I thought about staying at Jean-Mathias's apartment again tonight, but his couch, while very comfortable for sitting, isn't very comfortable for sleeping, and we both agreed we didn't want to rush things. Jean-Mathias might not be quite as rigid on the subject of sex as I am, but he agreed wholeheartedly that our relationship was worth doing right, and that means taking our time. It's one thing for a friend to crash on another friend's couch. It's another thing entirely for me to sleep in my boyfriend's bed the first night we're together, even if we have been best friends for months.

We're going skiing tomorrow.

I said something about Xavier, and Jean-Mathias shook his head. We might run into them on the slopes, but this isn't a group outing. This is a date. Could he be any more perfect for me? His idea of a date is to go skiing for the day. And when I suggested the play that's opening next weekend at one of the local theaters, he was just as excited about that. Matching interests.

I know all about opposites attracting and all that, but there has to be some common ground on which to base a relationship, and Jean-Mathias and I have that in spades. He drove me home, saying it was too cold for me to take the bus, but really I think he didn't want to let me go any more than I wanted to leave. He drove up in front of the Moreaus' house and we ended up sitting in the car, talking and kissing for another thirty minutes before I finally made myself go inside.

Comparing boyfriends is probably a really bad idea, but I don't have any other way to explain what I'm feeling at the moment. Kissing Pierre was sweet and romantic, kind of playful and tender, but it wasn't ground-shaking. Kissing Yves was definitely ground-shaking, but it was also about submitting to him. He wanted, not a submissive necessarily, but a bottom, a twink, someone who would give in to him at every turn. It's not that I have to be in charge all the time, but I don't want to always give in either.

Kissing Jean-Mathias is like coming home. It's sweet and romantic while at the same time with an edge that says it could be ground-shaking if we make it that way. If _we_ make it that way. That's the real beauty of it. Kissing Jean-Mathias is a partnership. It's something we do together, not something he does to me or me to him.

If everything else with Jean-Mathias is the same way, I have a feeling my hesitations will fade more quickly than I ever imagined possible. Only time will tell, but I really feel like this could be what I'm looking for.

So now we move forward together and see what happens. One step at a time, and all that, but together.

Wednesday, January 1

Happy New Year!

If New Year's Eve and New Year's Day are any indication of how my year will be, I'm in for a treat. Jean-Mathias and I went skiing as planned yesterday. We did actually run into Xavier and Stéphane on the slopes. They were surprised to see us so Romain apparently didn't tell them. Not that he knew we were going skiing, but they were surprised to see us together too.

We ate lunch with them in Courchevel and then skied together for a while before Jean-Mathias claimed jetlag as a reason to need to return to Grenoble early. That's one of the beauties of the season pass. You don't have to cram as much into a day as possible because you have five months to get your money's worth.

So we came home a little early. France doesn't have anything like Dick Clark or the ball falling in New York. Instead he made a traditional Réveillon meal and we shared it together at his apartment. We kissed at midnight as the bells tolled the new day and the new year. By that point we'd had too much to drink for him to drive me home (not as much as Monday night, but still too much for him to drive), so I caught a cab home. He picked me up this morning and we went to his family's house for a big holiday dinner. Since they didn't have their traditional Christmas celebration because of being in Africa, they decided to do it today. I wasn't sure about going, but Jean-Mathias insisted I'd be welcome as his friend even if I didn't feel comfortable telling them the rest yet.

I'm not ashamed of being in love with him, even if I haven't used those words yet, but it is still so new and so precious that I'm not completely ready to share it. He promised he understood, and so he introduced me as his meilleur ami (best friend) so there wouldn't be any confusion with the word copain. His parents were delighted to meet me, saying Jean-Mathias had told them so much about me.

Their house is beautiful. It's outside of Grenoble, in La Pérerrée. It's this tiny little commune. I bet there aren't 500 people in the entire town. And they have this absolutely beautiful crèche with hand-decorated figures (they call them santons here). It felt like Christmas. Christmas Eve and Christmas day with the Moreaus didn't really feel that way to me. I went to church, but the house wasn't really decorated or anything, and while they had a big meal and included me, the meal wasn't my traditional meal (not that the meal with the Pelissiers was my traditional meal either), and well, it just didn't feel like Christmas.

The meal with Jean-Mathias's family felt like Christmas. We had escargots to start, and then a goose stuffed with chestnuts, and so much food! But the best part was feeling like I was part of the family so quickly. It was Jean-Mathias's parents, his brother Charles, and his youngest sister Agathe. Obviously his other sister, Edwige, wasn't there since she just got married and she lives in Africa anyway.

Edwige is the oldest, followed by Charles, then Jean-Mathias, and then Agathe who started college in Nice this fall. Mme Pelissier (she asked me to call her Natalie, but I'm not sure I can do that yet) talked about how nice it was to have a full table again. They exchanged gifts in Africa so I didn't feel bad about not having anything other than the bouquet of flowers I brought for Mme Pelissier. It wasn't the gifts or even the decorations, really, that made it feel like Christmas. It was the feeling of family, which is odd because the Moreaus are a family, but this just felt different. Or maybe I felt different. Goodness knows it's been a roller coaster for the last month.

After we ate, we moved into the living room, which has this huge marble fireplace. M. Pelissier (François, if I can ever make myself use it) lit the traditional Yule log and we drank mulled wine and talked. Well, mostly they talked and I listened, but it still felt like I was part of the family, being included in all these wonderful family stories and jokes. Jean-Mathias sat next to me the whole time. I kept wanting to reach over and squeeze his hand or touch him or just connect with him somehow.

He must have read my mind because he finally put his arm around me. Nobody said anything or even seemed to notice, so either Jean-Mathias told them earlier or they figured it out on their own. Either way, as we were leaving, Mme Pelissier hugged me and told me she hoped to see me again soon.

I hugged her back and told her I would love to visit again as soon as the opportunity arose. Apparently it's Charles's birthday in two weeks. She invited me to come to the party with Jean-Mathias.

This is what was missing from my other relationships. The feeling of being connected to something larger than just the relationship. I told her I'd be delighted to attend and that I'd get the information from Jean-Mathias.

Jean-Mathias drove me home and dropped me off (with a few lingering kisses to hold me over until tomorrow), and I came back up here to write.

We'll have to figure out work still, but we have the weekend to do that. Honestly, most of the time we're too busy with our experiments to spend that much time together at work, other than lunch, so I doubt anything will change there. It's not like I'm planning on kissing him in the middle of lab. That would be totally unprofessional. We'll see how it goes, I guess.

Thursday, January 2

We went skiing again today and then back to Jean-Mathias's apartment for dinner. We made a raclette because we were cold and it was warm. The best part about a raclette? Other than cooking the potatoes and tossing together a salad, it's a cook-as-you-go meal. You melt the cheese on a grill at the table and pour it over the potatoes and cold cuts right there as you're ready for it. I bet it would be fun with a crowd, but it was really intimate for two as well. Jean-Mathias kept feeding me bites off his plate, as if I didn't have the exact same thing on mine.

It's like something flipped a switch inside both of us because when we were done eating, we couldn't keep our hands to ourselves. We ended up back on his couch, snuggled together, making out. There were still plenty of sweet, tender kisses, but there were also a few of those ground-shaking ones, the ones I knew would happen when we were ready for them. Apparently we were ready tonight.

I say apparently not because I question it, but because I hadn't consciously thought about it before it happened. It wasn't a decision I made so much as it was going with something that felt right when it happened. The best part is that thinking about it now, it still feels right. I don't think I'd realized how much some of what Yves and I did together really bothered me until I had an intimate moment that didn't leave me feeling that way.

We still stopped at kisses and touching through our clothes, so it's not everything I did with Yves, but there's no doubt now, no question as to whether this is right or whether I should be doing this.

We haven't talked about June yet because it's too soon, but I already know that I'm willing to look at all my options if this works out. This is too special to lose.

Sunday, January 5

It's back to work tomorrow. I'm not sure if that's good or bad. Mostly good. I like what I'm doing. It's interesting, and Dr. Besson has given me more and more control over the project as I've proven my abilities, and I've gotten some really interesting results. I'm looking forward to seeing what else comes of it as the year goes on. I can already see several different directions the project could go in. I'm going to have a hard time giving it up when it's time to go home.

Think Mom would kill me if I decided to stay?

Jean-Mathias and I have started making a list of places we should visit and things we should go to. Not that skiing every weekend isn't fun, because it is, but if I'm leaving in June, I should squeeze in as much as possible while I'm here.

For sure, we're going to the Carnaval de Nice in February. I even know about that, and I'm not French. He also mentioned a gypsy festival in Stes. Maries de la Mer in May. I mentioned wanting to visit the D-day beaches, which Jean-Mathias said he's never done. He suggested we should also visit the Loire valley and see the castles there.

So much to see.

With the weather as cold as it is right now, going north of us isn't really an option, so we've decided on Carcassonne for three weeks from now since Charles's birthday is in two weeks.

We got online and started searching for hotels.

Totally different from the trip with Yves where he took over everything.

We've made our hotel reservations for Jan. 24-26. Jean-Mathias suggested we see if Dr. Besson would let us flex our time that week or the week before so we could take Friday off and leave early, because it's a four-hour train ride or drive no matter how you cut it. I think we'll probably drive on this trip because that way we'd have the car to visit Toulouse or Albi or some of the areas around Carcassonne if we decide we want to, or we could leave early to come home and stop somewhere along the way. And if we stay in Carcassonne the whole weekend, that's okay, too, because it's the same length trip either way.

It's getting harder and harder to leave each evening. I wonder how long it will be before I stop fighting myself and stay. Because that's what I'm doing. My upbringing is warring with my heart, and so far my upbringing is winning because we haven't really been dating for a week yet, but so much happened to get us to this point that it feels like a lot longer. That's what my heart keeps telling me.

Not that Jean-Mathias has actually asked me to stay, but he hasn't asked me to leave. I'm always the one who looks at the clock and says it's time for me to go home. He agrees and drives me home, kissing me sweetly at the door and driving away.

The problem is that I'm afraid to trust my heart. I thought I was falling in love with Yves, and I let my heart lead me away from my beliefs, from my conscience, and I did things now I wish I hadn't.

Maybe Jean-Mathias will come with me to David et Jonathan this week and meet everyone there. Maybe that will help me feel better about everything. As much as I want Jean-Mathias to be the one, as much as I believe he is, a part of me isn't quite ready to put my full faith in that. I mean, come on, this is Jean-Mathias, the first friend I made here and the one who's always there when I need him, the one who's been my best friend since I got here. But I was wrong once before, well, twice if you count Pierre, but that one doesn't bother me as much. With Pierre, we chose to go our separate ways before I did anything to regret. We kissed a few times. I learned about wine. We went to the movies. Nothing to blush about or in any way regret.

When I think about Yves and letting him ~~touch me~~ use me the way I did, it makes me a little sick to my stomach.

I know Jean-Mathias wouldn't use me the same way, but that doesn't mean I'm ready for him to touch me that way either. Of course I'm getting ahead of myself because he hasn't given any indication of being ready for it either. And the hotel in Carcassonne does have two beds. It touched me that Jean-Mathias didn't assume we'd share a bed just because we're dating now.

Everything about him is different from Yves. I should trust that and stop worrying, but I can't seem to do that.

Maybe it's time to go to bed.

Monday, January 6

We made it through work without embarrassing ourselves or anyone else, although Paolo, our waiter, knows about us now. He came up to the table right as Jean-Mathias leaned over and kissed me. It wasn't a huge, long liplock or anything, more of a quick peck, but it was on the mouth so I don't think it could be mistaken for anything else. I'm cool with that. I want to be comfortable with that kind of little gesture.

I guess maybe I'm not as comfortable with it as I thought if I wrote it that way. Not 'I'm comfortable with that,' but I want to be comfortable with it. That has nothing to do with Jean-Mathias, actually. It's more a question of not knowing how the people around us will react and not wanting to cause a scene if they react badly.

I guess I'm not as over the homophobia of my upbringing as I thought I was. I certainly haven't been treated badly here in any situation where it was obvious I was gay. Nobody at the museum functions seemed bothered that I was there as Yves's date. I'll have to think about that, maybe even bring it up at David et Jonathan on Wednesday. I've accepted my sexuality, I've told my family and friends, I have a boyfriend, albeit a new one. So how do I get past hesitating every time I think about strangers realizing I'm gay? Or do I have to come out all over again every day?

That's kind of a depressing thought.

Not that coming out was terrible. Mom and Dad were sad, but they didn't kick me out or anything. They asked if I was sure, if I'd really thought this through. They wanted to know if they'd done something to make me this way. I think a lot of the typical questions parents probably have, especially conservative parents.

But I got a letter from home today, and Mom mentioned attending a PFLAG meeting. I was stunned. They might have been shocked and saddened, but they're not ignoring it. They aren't trying to keep me in the closet.

If they're making that kind of effort, I can too. I just have to figure out what the effort is.

Wednesday, January 8

Jean-Mathias went with me to David et Jonathan tonight. At first I was worried it would make it harder to have the discussion about my realization the other night and the whole issue of coming out, but it didn't, because when I hesitated or stumbled over what I wanted to say, he squeezed my hand in silent encouragement. It was such a wonderful feeling to know I wasn't alone.

Not that I've ever really felt alone at David et Jonathan, but this was different.

The answers I got were both frightening and encouraging.

Everyone agreed that coming out was a continuous process because people meet us and approach us with certain assumptions, namely that we're straight, and it's so easy to get sick to death of knowing the person they see and think they know is totally different from the person you are, and the only way to remedy those misassumptions is to tell them something that's really none of their business. They also said, though, that in some situations it doesn't matter. If the woman in the flower shop assumes I'm buying flowers for my girlfriend instead of my boyfriend, who cares? No, she shouldn't make assumptions, but it isn't a battle worth fighting, not when I'm going to spend a sum total of ten minutes in her presence.

On the other hand, if the HR director makes the assumption, I have to deal with it because if I want my partner to share my benefits, I have to declare him. Him, not her.

And they assured me it wouldn't take long for me to begin to recognize the difference.

That's certainly part of it, but the rest of it is in the simple living of my life. Kissing Jean-Mathias in the café or holding hands with him as we walk down the street. The answer was somewhat less clear-cut there because it wasn't a question of correcting a wrong assumption, but the reality is that I can either be proud of who I am and who I'm with or I can hide it. I promised myself I wouldn't go back in the closet, so I guess that means I have to let people see who I am unless I feel like I'm in a situation where doing so would be dangerous.

That's a little scary. I was a kid when Matthew Shepard was killed, and while I know gay bashing happens, I keep wanting to believe that things have gotten better since then. It's been over a decade. Surely things should be better by now, but I guess not entirely.

After David et Jonathan was over, Jean-Mathias drove me home and we ended up talking about it. He asked me if I was just now realizing how I instinctively mentioned or didn't mention things. He said he'd noticed it when I talked about Pierre and, to a lesser extent, Yves. I didn't bring it up at all at work, except with him, because I wasn't "out" at work. With the guys, though, I wasn't nearly as careful. I wasn't necessarily obvious about it, but I wasn't as hesitant either. And at Pole Étudiant, I was pretty much entirely in the closet. He said he never heard me say anything in that context that would even suggest I was gay. Not that I'd denied it. I'd just never corrected the assumptions they were surely all making. And I know they wouldn't judge me for it because they didn't judge Cristian for it.

He's right.

That gives me something else to think about. I'm not nearly as out as I think I am. I haven't ever denied being gay since coming to France. That's a start, but I haven't come nearly as far as I thought I had. Of course, up until now, I haven't had a reason to come out at work or at the Pole Étudiant. If everything works out with Jean-Mathias, that could change quickly.

And that's an awful lot of thinking for one paragraph. Maybe it's time to stop for tonight. I have to decide what to do now, but I'm too drained to make any decisions tonight. Because I have to decide whether it matters that I'm not really out at work or at Pole Étudiant, and that isn't as simple as waving my hand.

Friday, January 10

We're going skiing with the guys again this weekend. Xavier's family has a chalet for a week, and a bunch of us are going to crash on their floor tonight and tomorrow night to save the trip back and forth from Grenoble.

Jean-Mathias and I talked about the fact that we didn't want to hide from our friends. That doesn't mean we're going to sit and make out in front of them or anything, but I don't want to go an entire weekend without holding his hand or giving him a quick kiss, and Jean-Mathias agreed. He said the guys pretty much all know about him. In fact when he first brought me to play football, Romain asked later if we were dating and Jean-Mathias told him no. It was the truth at the time, just not now, so he doesn't think the guys will have any problem with us being together.

I'm a little nervous, but ~~I can't~~ I won't let that fear rule or ruin my life. I don't know if Xavier's parents will be there and how they'll feel about it, but that's less important in the long run than how Xavier and the guys feel. If they're not cool with it, it could make Sunday afternoons uncomfortable or impossible.

Jean-Mathias assures me we have nothing to worry about, and honestly I think he's right. It's the whole coming out again thing. I did this already. Okay, it's time to get ready for work. I'm all packed. We'll just stop by on the way out of town to grab my bag and my skis.

We didn't get to Courchevel in time to ski tonight, but we did make it in time to have fondu with Xavier's family. Yum. That's all I have to say about that.

No, not really. Like the raclette (which Xavier said would probably be tomorrow's dinner), it's a cook-at-the-table meal that creates a real sense of camaraderie. Something about having to take your time over the meal, maybe. And of course every time you lose a piece of bread in the cheese, you have to take a drink. Some of us (me) were pretty loose by the end of the meal. After we ate and cleaned up, we all moved into the living room with its huge fireplace and settled around it. The chalet doesn't have a TV, which I found surprising, but Xavier said they deliberately get one without so they can spend this time together as a family without worrying about TV or the computer or anything like that taking their attention away.

That's actually really a neat idea.

So we sat around the living room laughing and talking. Before long, I realized I was leaning against Jean-Mathias. I must have tensed because almost immediately, he put his arm lightly around my waist, steadying me and keeping me in place. I don't know if nobody noticed (which is possible) or if nobody cared (which is more likely), but the sky didn't fall, hell didn't freeze over, and pigs didn't fly. It was about as anticlimactic as coming out could be, I think. Just the way it should be, Jean-Mathias reminded me when I made that observation to him before bed.

We're all stretched out in sleeping bags on the floor of various rooms. Jean-Mathias, Romain, and I are in the living room. They're already asleep, but I had to write a little bit first. We'll be up early to get in a full day of skiing, and I didn't want to miss writing down these thoughts.

They're too important to let pass that way. Coming out doesn't have to be some big, tense, drama-filled moment, and I think I expected it always would be, which is rather ridiculous when I think about how I came out to Jean-Mathias. Of course, he's gay too, even if he didn't say anything at the time, so maybe it isn't the same, but I think it's time to let the drama go. I'm sure there will be plenty of it at different times, but maybe I really can expect things to be less difficult than I feared.

Sunday, January 12

I'm so sore it hurts just sitting here, and walking is agony.

We had a blast on Saturday, and Sunday was fabulous right up until the moment I went face down, skis up in the snow. I think I pulled something in my thigh. Seriously. The entire inside of my left thigh aches and if I try to stretch at all, that only makes it worse. Xavier's dad is a doctor, and he said ice and ibuprofen. The ibuprofen is easy. The ice is miserable because it's cold in Grenoble too, and even with the radiator on full, I can't seem to get warm at night these days. The ice is only making it worse.

Jean-Mathias said he'd pick me up for work tomorrow so I don't have to change buses or walk as far with my leg hurting.

I swear, if something can go wrong, it will.

I'm going to get another ice pack, take two more Advil, and try to sleep.

Wednesday, January 15

I'm still limping a little, although it's better than it was on Monday. Tonight is Pole Étudiant, the first one since Jean-Mathias and I started dating. We still haven't decided what we're doing tonight. I mean, we're going, but we haven't decided whether we're going to let anyone know we're together.

Hell, for all I know, they all think we're together anyway. That's what Romain thought when he first met me.

There aren't really any couples in the group that I'm aware of, or if there are, they choose to be discreet during dinner and the discussion, so it's not like I'm planning on hanging all over Jean-Mathias anyway. Not because of the coming out part, but because that's not the place for that kind of behavior. I think I'll suggest correcting any wrong assumptions and leaving it at that. Maybe that's a cop out, but it's that discussion about the battles worth fighting. I'm not sure it's worth making a scene at Pole Étudiant if they aren't actively trying to make us straight.

That doesn't even make sense.

If the subject doesn't come up, I don't see the need to bring it up. Oh, and by the way, I'm gay. Why do they need to know that if it isn't relevant to our discussions? Nobody's bashing homosexuality. If they start, that's different, but if the conversation is about the role of the saints in our everyday lives, I don't see where homosexuality fits into that.

Does that make me a bad gay man?

I don't think so. I guess we'll see if Jean-Mathias disagrees.

He didn't disagree, fortunately. I'm not sure he would have made the same choice if I hadn't been in the picture, but he knows I'm struggling with this. I love that he's letting me figure it out at my own pace and comfort level instead of pushing me to fit his idea of where I should be in this process.

Kind of the same way he's letting me find my own pace where the physical side of our relationship is concerned. I told him the day we started dating what I had done and not done with Yves, and I told him I wished things hadn't gone as far as they did. He promised me then that he wouldn't ever pressure me into anything I wasn't ready for. He might ask, at times, if I wanted something, but I shouldn't ever feel like

I had to say yes. So far he hasn't even asked. Our kisses get more intense with each passing day, but he hasn't pressed for more.

This weekend is his brother's birthday. We're going to La Pérerrée for the weekend. Jean-Mathias assured me his mother had suggested it and offered me Edwige's room for the stay. That takes care of my concerns about sleeping with him. I only hope his extended family is as accepting as his immediate family is.

I have got to stop worrying about this. Jean-Mathias wouldn't have suggested it and his mother wouldn't have invited me if I weren't welcome.

I'm going to bed.

Saturday, January 18

I really shouldn't have worried. Everyone has been as kind as could be. Jean-Mathias only has one grandparent left, and I don't know if she picked up on our relationship. She seemed a little out of it, but everyone else has been lovely and welcoming. The party itself reminds me a lot of Pierre's party, in terms of the multiple courses and all the rest. I guess the difference is how comfortable I am now in my own skin and in France. I'm not worried as much about saying the wrong thing or screwing up and using an informal when I should use a formal (or vice versa, although that isn't quite as serious). I still always start with the formal tone and let the person I'm talking to invite me to informality because I don't want to offend, but it feels more natural now than it did six months ago when I first arrived.

The sun was out today, so even though it was cold, we went for a walk in the country lanes, and let me tell you, there is nothing out here but mountains and trees. I think I overestimated that 500 for the population. I think there are about ten houses total. Anyway, everyone except the grandmother went for a walk, everyone just being together. The couples were all holding hands, and about halfway down the mountain, Jean-Mathias reached for mine. It was wonderful to be part of the family and just act just like everyone else and not have to justify our choices.

Of course maybe they're waiting until I've gone to bed or have gone home to demand an explanation. Good breeding and all that, but it didn't feel that way.

And now I'm curled back up in Edwige's bed, trying to get warm (because I can't seem to stay warm at night) and wishing we could stay longer.

~~Mme Pelissier~~ Natalie said the family would drive into Domène tomorrow for Mass if I'd like to come with them. I told her I'd love to go with them, even if Jean-Mathias slept in. She assured me he wouldn't.

Someone's at my door.

It was Jean-Mathias coming to see if I needed anything and if I'd had a good day. He snuggled under the covers with me to help warm me up while we talked for a bit. Yes, all we did was talk and kiss a little. I wouldn't disrespect his mother's house (or his sister's bed!) that way. Even if we were sleeping together sometimes, I'd still take the extra bed at his mother's house until we were actually ready to make a long-term commitment. That's the way I was raised.

So we talked about the day and his family and tomorrow and next weekend. And snuggled together until we were in danger of falling asleep. It would have been easy to sleep that way. He was warm, and now that he's gone, I'm cold again, but it wouldn't have been right. He agreed. Reluctantly, but he agreed, kissed me good night, and went back to his room.

Of course now I'm awake again instead of almost asleep. The price I pay for listening to my conscience, I guess. It's better than the price I paid for not listening to it.

Friday, January 24

We're on our way to Carcassonne. Jean-Mathias is driving now, but I promised I'd drive some later. I won't write much in the car probably, because I'd rather talk to him, but I wanted to at least write something since I haven't written all week. We've spent pretty much every evening together, to the point that Mme Moreau offered to decrease my rent a little if I wasn't going to be eating with them anymore, so I wouldn't be paying twice. I told her I wasn't quite ready to commit to that yet, but that I'd let her know if I reached that point.

And when I have gotten home, it's been so late that all I've done is climb into bed and go to sleep. It's still miserably cold so I don't even want to sit in bed and write. Jean-Mathias has the heat cranked all the way up in the car for me, even if he's teasing me about having thin blood. I reminded him I came from Texas and could count on one hand the number of times I'd seen snow before moving to Grenoble. And yes, I love skiing, but I also love coming inside somewhere <u>warm</u> when I'm done, and it seems like the definition of warm in houses here isn't the same as at home.

Jean-Mathias wants my attention. I'll write more later.

I've figured out the solution to the cold.

Cassoulet.

It's a traditional dish in southwestern France in the area around Carcassonne. It's this incredibly thick bean stew, almost a casserole it's so thick, with duck, goose, and partridge meat in it. The kind of meal that sticks to your ribs and keeps you warm all night. Pair that with a hearty glass of red wine and I'm actually warm for the first time, it feels like, since Jean-Mathias went back to his own bed last Saturday night.

We obviously made it to Carcassonne with no problem. We got here early enough to take advantage of a bit of sunshine and wander the ramparts before it started getting dark and too cold to be outside. That's when we went into a restaurant and he convinced me to try the cassoulet.

The city is amazing. Parts of the fortifications date all the way back to Roman times, with the bulk of the fortifications being built during the twelfth and thirteenth centuries. It's the largest double-walled city in Europe. A real medieval fortress. It was actually only taken in battle once, well before the current fortifications were built. Obviously it wouldn't do much against modern weapons, but in the Middle Ages, it was impregnable. The Lower Town (the part outside the fortifications) was ransacked more than once, but not the fortified section of town. It's up on top of a hill right above the Aude river, rising up out of the plain. It's lit up at night. Jean-Mathias tried to convince me to go walking through the Lower Town tonight so we could see it, but I'm actually warm and the thought of going back out in the cold really doesn't appeal. Maybe tomorrow night.

He laughed at me when I said that, like I'll be any happier about the cold tomorrow than I am tonight. Maybe we can go see it before we have dinner tomorrow. Then we can have cassoulet again and I can stay warm during the night. It still gets dark so early. By five o'clock, it's getting dark. At home, it's light until seven, maybe even a little later, and most restaurants here don't start serving dinner until close to seven, so we could walk out and look at the ramparts, then come back inside the walls for dinner.

I'm starting to get cold so I'm going to climb in bed and let the covers keep the chill away.

Saturday, January 25

I shared a bed with Jean-Mathias last night.

I wasn't planning on it. We got a double room without even discussing it. And then last night after I got in my own bed, I felt odd with him in the other bed, like I needed to justify my choice, which is silly since he didn't say anything or ever suggest we should sleep in the same bed. Anyway, I told him he mattered too much to me for me to rush into things with him the way I'd done with Yves. Even knowing Jean-Mathias the way I do, I still expected his answer to be like Yves's always was, reminding me not to expect him to wait forever. Instead Jean-Mathias told me to take all the time I needed, that he would rather I be sure than regret anything we did together.

That did it.

I kept saying Yves wasn't pressuring me, but he really was, just subtly. Jean-Mathias's answer is really what no pressure feels like. And that's what let me put aside my hesitations and change beds. We both stayed dressed in our pajamas. All we did was kiss a couple of times before falling asleep, but I woke up a couple of times during the night with his arm draped over me, and it felt so right.

And I wasn't cold at all during the night.

I'm sure I'll be cold when we go outside today, but the memory of last night should provide some extra warmth, along with hoping for a repeat tonight.

Jean-Mathias is in the shower now, then it'll be my turn. We did this in Lyon, sharing a room this way, but it feels different now. When we were in Lyon, I spent my time thinking about Pierre. Now I'm thinking about the fact that Jean-Mathias is wet and naked on the other side of that door. Not exactly conducive to sitting here calmly writing in my journal.

The thing is, I like the idea of that, but I'm not ready to walk in there and join him.

Gulp.

I wasn't ready for him to walk out of there in just a towel either because he forgot his boxers. I've seen him at the pool (and his Speedos are smaller than the towel), but this was different, way more intimate because it's just us and it's a towel. I think I need to go kiss my boyfriend.

That turned into more than just a kiss. I've had a shower and Jean-Mathias is taking another one. I kissed him, and he kissed me back, and we ended up rubbing up against each other there in the bathroom, him pressed up against the door, and he was as hard as I was, and we just kept kissing and grinding and his skin was so hot and damp and I could smell the cologne he'd just put on and yeah. He's taking another shower, and I'll have to sleep in my jeans tonight because my pajama bottoms have to be washed before I can wear them again.

How am I going to keep my hands to myself tonight when I know how good it feels to touch him now?

He's done with his shower. I should see what he wants to do today.

We decided to drive over to Toulouse for the day. La Ville Rose, they call it, because so much of the city is built with reddish brick instead of the more typical yellow limestone. It's also the center of the French aerospace industry, but that isn't nearly as interesting to me as the old town, with its donjon and all the other medieval, Renaissance, and classical buildings.

And we got to see Carcassonne by night as we drove back into town, so I don't even have to go out in the cold to see it lit up. Jean-Mathias was right. It was worth the view, and it would have been worth going back out and getting cold again to see it, but this way I don't have to. We can hurry down the street to the restaurant we decided to try tonight and get dinner. And then hurry back and get in bed.

Jean-Mathias is ready to go.

Jean-Mathias wouldn't let me order cassoulet again. He said I had to try some of the other regional specialties too. So I had foie gras (which was so much better than I ever imagined liver could be), roast squab, and this amazing melted chocolate creation. It wasn't quite as stick to your ribs as the cassoulet, but definitely delicious, and since I'm curled up next to Jean-Mathias, the cold isn't nearly as much of an issue. He's flipping channels on the TV while I write. He isn't even trying to distract me.

I don't think it ever occurred to me to write while I was with Yves. After the fact, yes, but not while we were actually together. I don't know if that has anything to do with Yves himself or more with the fact that our time together was so much more limited and structured. Even when we traveled to Paris, he wanted all of my attention all of the time unless my attention was on something he directed it to, like the play. With Jean-Mathias, simply being together is enough. I'm sure he wouldn't like it if I never did anything but write while we were together, but it isn't like that. I write when he's in the shower or doing something else or when we're relaxing before bed.

Mmm… TV just went off. More tomorrow.

Sunday, January 26

I'm home. We decided to leave early and stop in Nîmes and Orange on the way home, to see the Roman buildings there. I'm sure there's much more to do in both cities, but in Nîmes, we visited the coliseum, the baths, and the Maison Carrée, which was a Roman temple before becoming a church, then a meeting hall, and now a museum. Then in Orange we stopped to see the outdoor theater, which is one of the few in the world that still has the stage wall intact. It always amazes me what the Romans were able to accomplish. I wonder sometimes where our technology would be if the empire hadn't fallen the way it did, leading to the Dark Ages.

It feels odd to be back in my bed by myself after sleeping next to Jean-Mathias the last two nights. I didn't feel like I could just not come home, though, after I told Mme Moreau to expect me home this evening. I had dinner with them tonight. Elodie immediately claimed my attention for help with her English work. She's gotten so much better as we've worked on things over the fall semester, but the work also keeps getting harder so she still needs help sometimes.

I feel a little bad for neglecting her over the past month. I'll have to talk to Jean-Mathias about that. Serge hasn't seemed to need the help as much, but Elodie and I have spent some hours together, and I did promise I'd help when she needed it. Maybe I should talk with her and with Jean-Mathias about finding a night when I'm always home to help with stuff. The only problem with that is if something comes up in between, but while I do want to help her, I'm not willing to give up my time with Jean-Mathias either.

It's already weird not to sleep next to him. I can't imagine not having dinner with him, at least most nights. We need to talk about this, I suspect, because I don't know how he feels about the idea of me staying over sometimes. Not moving in. Just spending the occasional Friday or Saturday night when we aren't traveling. We're going to Nice in a couple of weeks for Carnaval, but we don't have anything planned between now and then. It's not like we can travel every weekend anyway. Our salaries only go so far.

I guess this begs the question of how soon is too soon to move in together. I know the answer is that it's still too soon, but at what point isn't it too soon? How do I know when I'm ready and when it's the right step for our relationship?

More questions, as always. It seems like every time I get the answer to one, twenty more pop up.

I'm not going to find the answers tonight, though. I'll go to sleep and dream of what it felt like to have Jean-Mathias's arms around me during the night and his kisses nuzzling me awake in the morning.

Saturday, February 1

I spent the night with Jean-Mathias last night. It wasn't planned, so I'm feeling a little grungy in day-old clothes, but we had dinner and started talking and suddenly it was well after midnight. Jean-Mathias offered to drive me home, but we'd been drinking and it was obvious he was exhausted. It didn't feel fair (or safe) to make him drive, and I didn't have enough cash for a cab, so I stayed. After last weekend, it seemed silly to sleep on the couch.

We had a little repeat of last Saturday too, only in bed instead of against the wall. And with more hands. And more time.

I shouldn't be so hung up over the sex, but after the mistakes I made with Yves, every step feels fraught now with the possibility of screwing things up again. It didn't feel wrong, though. It felt good to be touched, and not just my body. My heart feels good today and so does my mind. I don't feel guilty about this like I did with Yves.

And I found I like lying on top of Jean-Mathias even more than I like having him lying on top of me. Not that I dislike lying beneath him. I don't. It felt amazing to have his weight pressing me into the mattress, but I kind of liked pressing him into the mattress too, especially when he bucked up against me and came in his boxers.

Come to think of it, I had him pressed against the door in Carcassonne too. Now isn't that interesting? Something else to think about. When he isn't calling me to come eat breakfast. I could get used to this really fast.

It was raining today so we spent most of the day inside, watching TV, reading, talking.

Making out.

I sound like a sex fiend, but it's so much more than that. Yes, we went back to bed for a cuddle this afternoon and it turned into another hot and heavy frottage session, but that was an hour out of our day together. The rest of the time was spent doing other things or just being together. That's what Yves and I never did. We never just spent time together without something else to do or without it turning sexual.

After our nap we finally decided to go to the pool so we could get a little exercise, but even that ended up more joking than anything else as we mock raced each other. We were the only ones in the pool, so we ended up horsing around instead of swimming all that much. It was still good to get out of the house. Tomorrow Jean-Mathias promised we'd go for a real swim if the weather was too bad to go skiing.

Afterward, we went by the Moreaus so I could change clothes. I grabbed another change of clothes just in case. I don't know if I'll stay again tonight, but this way I have clean clothes if I do. It's just so easy and comfortable and I keep looking for the catch.

That's the part of everything with Yves I regret the most. Instead of believing in the happiness I've found, I keep searching for a downside, a reason to hold back or pull away, like I have to protect my heart from Jean-Mathias. I know that's ridiculous. I know he wouldn't treat me that way, but I can't seem to get that knowledge to penetrate at a gut level. I only wish I knew what it would take. I'd do it, or ask Jean-Mathias to do it, in a heartbeat if I did.

I guess it's a matter of time and letting the constant care soak in until I simply can't doubt anymore.

Dinner's ready.

Sunday, February 2

I stayed the night again. I couldn't make myself bring up leaving and Jean-Mathias didn't mention it either. It got to be midnight, and he looked at me and said, "Let's go to bed." So we did.

We started kissing and rubbing because it feels so good, but suddenly I wanted more. I hate to say I didn't ask, but I didn't even think about it. I just reached between us and started stroking him. I could tell he was surprised, but I don't think he minded. He certainly didn't act like he minded.

When he slid his hand inside my shorts and returned the favor, I thought I'd died and gone to heaven. And then when he was done (and I was so beautifully done that I felt like I'd never move again), he licked his hand clean instead of going to get a washcloth. I swear, I got hard all over again.

I'm so in love with him. I know that isn't news, but every time we're together, I fall a little harder. I keep thinking it's too soon to tell him that because we only started dating a month ago, but it feels like the six months leading up to that were all part of it too, and seven months maybe isn't too fast.

Thursday, February 6

I found a minute at David et Jonathan yesterday to see if Claude would be free for coffee this afternoon after work. He was, fortunately, and so we spent some time discussing everything that's happened since last month and all the questions I didn't want to bring up in the group discussion last night with Jean-Mathias sitting beside me. It's not that I want to hide my feelings from him, but until I know the answer to my own questions, I don't want to get his hopes up.

Claude agreed that my friendship with Jean-Mathias added depth and stability to our relationship and that under the circumstances, while he wouldn't recommend rushing into anything, if I was sure of my feelings, it wasn't too soon to say something. We are adults, old enough to know our minds. We're at a position in our lives where we can make rational decisions and stick by them, Jean-Mathias even more than me since he's twenty-six.

The rest of this, the part I can't forget, is that if I want this to last beyond June, I can't wait until then to make plans, at least not without having to go home first. My job and my visa expire. Dr. Besson might be willing to hire me on full-time or to help me find someone in the area who would if he can't, but that takes time, and I'd have to apply for an extension of my work visa, and that has to start at least two months before my current one expires.

So maybe the solution isn't to base this decision on a permanent commitment but instead on my desire to see what could come of this. Yes, it would mean deferring graduate school another year or possibly even having to reapply if I return to the US, but if I stay here permanently, I'd either want to go to graduate school here or maybe I wouldn't need the advanced degree. That would be a question for Dr. Besson.

I guess I need to schedule a meeting with my mentor to see what he considers my options to be. Then I need to have a serious talk with Jean-Mathias to see which, if any, of those options I should take.

There's Jean-Mathias. He had an experiment run over. I'll write more later.

Friday, February 7

I went in to schedule a meeting with Dr. Besson and he had time to talk right then. I explained about wanting to stay on in France on a longer-term basis, although I didn't mention Jean-Mathias's name. This has to be about me and doing what's right for me, even if what's right for me is having time to explore my relationship with him. Dr. Besson said if I wanted a job, I could certainly stay on as a tech in his lab, but that if I wanted a real career, I should consider enrolling in a doctoral program here. I could keep working with him as I do it, but it would mean student status again instead of a salary. Of course school here is a whole lot cheaper than it would be at home, so that's an advantage. It would mean reevaluating my finances, though, or else having Jean-

Mathias willing to help support me for the time it would take to get my degree. The other option would be to work for a year or two and save up enough money to be able to then go back to school. That isn't the way it's usually done here, but that doesn't mean I can't do it.

So now I have to talk to Jean-Mathias, tell him what I'm thinking about, and see how he feels about it. And then I have to call Mom and tell her. She won't be happy, but I paid my way over here and I'm supporting myself while I'm here, so it's not like she can do anything except be unhappy. This is my choice to make and I have to make the one that's best for me. When I started this journal, I talked about this being a once-in-a-lifetime experience, to come live in France for a year. And it has been an amazing year so far (and it's not over yet!), but the real once in a lifetime may well be this relationship with Jean-Mathias. Mom will probably ask if I'm sure I don't want to come home and meet some nice American boy, but honestly, I don't. I'm ready to stay here and be with Jean-Mathias and see if he really is my once-in-a-lifetime love.

I guess that means I need to tell him I love him, doesn't it?

It's Friday. I packed a bag so I don't have to worry about even the pretense of going home. I'll tell him this weekend.

Saturday, February 8

How does one lead up to a declaration of love? I've spent the entire day trying to find the right way or moment to say it, with no luck. It's almost bedtime again. I mean, it's not the end of the world if I don't say it this weekend. I know that. I've already made my decision, unless Jean-Mathias says he doesn't want me, but I don't want to commit to another year if there's no chance of anything more than this coming from our relationship. If he doesn't think we can make these few months into a lifetime, then there's no reason to stay because I'll already know what we can have between us.

This is stupid. I'm going in there right now and telling him how I feel.

Sunday, February 9

Why was I worried again?

Jean-Mathias said he'd been trying to hold back because he knew I was leaving in a few months and it didn't seem fair to ask me to give up all my plans back at home, and so while he had enjoyed our time together, he was trying not to pressure me, especially after knowing what happened with Yves.

After I walked into the living room and blurted out that I'd fallen in love with him (and after he told me he felt the same and we kissed until we were breathless), we talked late into the night. He asked me about graduate school and all my plans and my career. I told him I'd talked to Dr. Besson and what he said my options were from where he was sitting. Jean-Mathias couldn't believe I'd already talked to him, but like I explained, I didn't know when I'd be ready to say something to him, and it was important enough to give us this chance that I would have done it unless Jean-Mathias said he didn't want to stay with me.

When we were finally talked out, at least for last night, we went to bed, and Jean-Mathias made love to me. It's not that what we did was all that different than previous nights. It's more the feeling behind it. It seems like every time he kissed me, he whispered "Je t'aime," and every time he said it, his voice got deeper, huskier, more intense. And every time I heard it, I believed it that much more.

I need to call home tonight, when it's late enough for Mom and Dad to be home from church. I don't know what will happen for sure with the job situation or even with Jean-Mathias and me, but I need to tell them this is happening. They'll say what they want to say, but I need to tell them.

It's not quite as good a story as Mom coming home from her best friend's wedding and announcing she'd met the man she was going to marry, but that's what I hope our outcome will be, and I owe it to my parents to share that with them.

Mom cried.

I think I may have cried with her a little, to tell the truth, but while I understand her tears, I can't let that sway me. And she did listen, even through her tears, when I told her I'd met a wonderful man who loves me and who I love. She asked about him and his family. I told her everything except the sex part. She doesn't want to hear that anyway.

Then she asked what our options are here. So I told her a little about the PACS, what little I know anyway, that it's a civil union open to straight or homosexual couples. She asked if we'd set a date. I told her we weren't at that point yet, that I was trying to stay so we could see if we were ready to get to that point. I think that reassured her, honestly, to hear that we aren't rushing blindly into something instead of taking our time and making sure it's the right thing for both of us. Because while Mom might have come home and announced she'd met the man she was going to marry, they dated for two years before they finally got engaged and almost another year after that before they finally got married, because they both understood it was forever and they didn't want to do something that couldn't be undone until they were sure it was the right decision.

A PACS can be undone. I know that, but it goes back to the covenant idea we've discussed so often at David et Jonathan. Legally it's a PACS because that's what our legal option is in France, but in our hearts it's a covenant as binding and sacred as any marriage vow. If we're going to make it, it needs to be the right decision.

Thursday, February 13

I spoke with Dr. Besson today and told him I'd like to stay on as a lab tech for now, that I might look into an advanced degree in a year or two, after I have my feet under me financially to be able to pay my living expenses while still going to school. He said he'd start filling out the paperwork to renew my carte de séjour and also suggested I start looking for an apartment since the original arrangement with the Moreaus was only for a year. He said it wasn't always easy to find a decent apartment at a reasonable price and it would be better to start now than to end up without a place to live.

I told him I already had a lead on a place. He looked impressed. I didn't give him details. When I finally move in with Jean-Mathias (and yes, we talked about it in the abstract without discussing when that would happen), I'll tell him, since it will be in my personnel file anyway. Until then it's not something he needs to know.

In other news, we've finalized all our plans for our trip to Nice next weekend. I can't wait. It's supposed to be a party to rival Mardi Gras in New Orleans. Not that I've been to Mardi Gras, but I've heard about it and seen pictures.

Now we just have to wait for it to be next weekend.

Friday, February 21

We're on the train on our way to Nice. We decided not to drive even though it isn't that far because of all the people who will be there. We weren't sure we'd be able to find parking, and this way we don't have to worry about it. We'll take the bus from the train station to the hotel, walk around the city while we're there, and take the bus back to the train station on Sunday to come home.

It's going to be so much fun. The parades and the dancing in the streets… being able to dance with Jean-Mathias in the streets. We went to the July 14 party together, but we weren't "together" so we didn't dance with each other. There won't be anything to stop us from dancing together this time.

Jean-Mathias found us a little tiny hotel near the parade route. It's probably a dump, but it's convenient and it's not like we'll spend much time there except to sleep. Well, and maybe a few other things, but still only at night. And furthermore it's only for two nights. Even if it truly is miserable, we can live with it for such a short time.

We made it to Nice in time to drop our bags off at the hotel (it's nicer than I expected) and head out to the opening ceremonies with the amazing parade and the floats, and I don't even know how to describe it except to say it was the most festive event I think I've ever been to. Even the Pride parade. We're back at the hotel. Jean-Mathias wanted a quick shower before bed so I'm using the time alone to write for a moment. Not that I have anything really useful to say other than raving about the Carnaval, but even that is an impression I don't want to lose. We made it down here this year. We may not make it next year. We may never make it down here again. This way I have some little note to remind myself of the event.

Saturday, February 22

What is it about giving a blow job that wigs me out so much?

I'd convinced myself it was because I felt pressured with Yves that I freaked out the last time, but Jean-Mathias didn't pressure me. If anything, I pressured myself.

Maybe I should start at the beginning. We went to bed after Jean-Mathias finished his shower, and that went about the way that always goes, with us kissing and snuggling and squirming out of what little we wore in the way of clothes, which wasn't much more than our boxers at that point. He smelled so good, like sandalwood and I don't know what else, and I couldn't keep my hands to myself. We kept kissing and touching, hands all over each other. It felt so good. And I could smell him. Not his soap, but him, and it smelled so good that all I wanted to do was cover myself in it. I kissed my way down his chest (and have I mentioned what a really, really fine chest it is?) and the smell just got stronger. He didn't say anything, didn't try to guide me. He just let me go at my own pace. I got all the way down to his dick and rubbed all over it with my face, which he really seemed to like judging by the noises he was making, but when I went to actually take him in my mouth, I couldn't do it. I froze, hanging there like an idiot.

I half-expected him to grab my head like Yves did. I know, not the same man, not the same situation, but I couldn't have been any more of a tease. I didn't mean to do it. I started with every intention of giving him a blow job, but I couldn't do it.

I don't get it. I don't mind touching him. I can't count the number of times we've used our hands to get each other off. So it isn't the idea of being intimate or making him come or him making me come. It isn't a lack of certainty where my feelings are concerned. I love him and I know he loves me. If he didn't, he wouldn't have been nearly as understanding last night, because unlike Yves, he didn't make any attempt to pressure me into following through. He pulled me back into his arms, kissed me, and told me we didn't ever have to do anything I wasn't comfortable with, and that he wouldn't enjoy it if I wasn't having a good time too. And then he rolled me onto my back and put his mouth on me. When he finished and I could breathe again, I jerked him off, but I felt like I'd given him the short end of the stick. He didn't make me feel that way. He pulled me against him and told me he loved me and how good I made him feel when I touched him and how much it meant to him that I trusted him enough to let him touch me and that I was confident enough to experiment even when I found I wasn't as comfortable as I thought I would be.

It reassured me last night that I hadn't screwed things up, but I have to get my head around this. I don't want to keep feeling like I can't love him like he loves me. It didn't bother him last night, but how long will that be the case? How long can I keep chickening out before he gets tired of my ignorance?

It's not the taste. I've tasted him off my fingers before. I won't say it's the best thing I've ever tasted (that would be the magret de canard aux cérises), but it's hardly the worst either. A little bitter, a little salty, but not disgusting or anything.

I think it's the whole "come in my mouth" thing. That's a lot to handle. Not to mention that he's not exactly small. I'm afraid I'll choke and look like an idiot or else gag myself and ruin the mood. The solution to that is to not let him go too deep. I mean, when he did me, he didn't deep throat me (is that the right term?) the entire time. Mostly he sucked on the tip, just going farther a few times. Most of the time, his hand took care of the rest of me. (Can you see me blushing and squirming? This is ridiculous. I'm twenty-two, nearly twenty-three, not fourteen.) And he knows I've never done this before. He isn't going to expect perfection, if there is such a thing. He's going to expect me to be as sloppy and hesitant and awkward as our first few hand jobs were. But I've gotten better at that. I know how to touch him now to make him feel good, and every time it seems to get easier, more comfortable.

I guess maybe I need to stop worrying and start. Even if I start small. A few licks or something, to get used to it. He'll let me take my time. He proved that yesterday far beyond my wildest dreams.

Now I just have to get up the courage to try again. Maybe tonight. He's stirring now, which means breakfast and a day at the Carnaval. The Bataille des Fleurs doesn't start until two-thirty, but I'm sure there will be something going on earlier. And if I'm wrong, maybe I'll work up my nerve sooner rather than later.

I'm back to being speechless again. We went to the Bataille des Fleurs, which isn't a battle at all, but a parade of floats lushly decorated with flowers of every possible shade and variety. It looked like a fairy garden come to life with all the costumes and characters on and around the floats. Truly magical. We ate and wandered and watched the parade and then went back for the Corso illuminé, another parade but at night this time, lit up with spotlights and neon, and it sounds tawdry, but it was such a festival. Yeah, this weekend has been a success on the tourist front, that's for sure. Now to see if I can make it a success on the personal front as well.

Maybe I should wait, but I'm afraid it's like getting thrown from a horse. If you don't get back on right away, it gets harder and harder to make yourself get back on later. I've had enough to drink today. Maybe it'll be Dutch courage and all.

Sunday, February 23

I don't know that blow jobs will ever be my favorite thing to do to a lover, but at least I know I can give one when I choose to. At least enough of one. I still finished Jean-Mathias off with my hands, but at least I got past the block that wouldn't even let me put my mouth on him.

And if that doesn't reduce a beautiful interlude to its basest terms, I don't know what would. You'd think I didn't have a romantic bone in my body, except I don't really know how to describe it without making it sound like a cheesy porno flick. I'll have to think about that, but later, because Jean-Mathias is pulling me back toward bed.

We're on the train heading home after another spectacular parade this afternoon. In addition to the floats, lots of the attendees wore costumes as well, from fairly simple ones that would fit right in with what you see little kids wearing for Halloween to some really elaborate ones that were as good or better than the ones in the parade. Jean-Mathias told me those are probably people who come every year and so have spent time and money putting together a costume they use repeatedly. It makes sense.

It's going to be a bit of a shock going back to Grenoble. It was in the teens in Nice (I actually wrote that without having to think it meant in the fifties at home! I'm integrating!), but it's still hovering near freezing at home. I'll have to snuggle close to Jean-Mathias to stay warm. Like that's any hardship.

So anyway, I was trying to write about last night (and this morning) without making it sound tawdry. Not succeeding, but trying.

The thing I realized last night is that making love with Jean-Mathias isn't about who touches who where or how or with what body part. It's about the emotion behind it. Whether I give him a partial blow job and finish him off with my hands or whether I kiss and rub against him until we both come that way, or some other combination, it doesn't matter because we're together and making each other feel good and showing each other how much we love one another, and that's far more important than whose hand went where. I'd love him just as much (and feel just as loved) if he'd put his hand somewhere else or if I had.

That may be the most freeing revelation I've had in some time. It isn't about what we do; it's about why we do it. Whether we spoon together and fall asleep or drive each other to screaming climaxes, it's the fact that we love each other that matters.

I got home to the Moreaus to a note from Mme Moreau that Mom had called while I was in Nice. I called her back, and she told me she and Dad are coming to visit. This weekend. They decided they want to meet Jean-Mathias and nothing would do but to do so immediately. I am so screwed.

Monday, February 24

I told Jean-Mathias about my parents today. He asked me what the big deal was. I've met his parents. Why shouldn't he meet mine?

Because my parents don't speak French, first of all, and because my parents only barely get the fact that I'm gay, and even trying to be supportive, they're bound to end up being insensitive. And because Mom jumps to conclusions, like asking if we'd already set a date, and that's embarrassing, and this is just a disaster waiting to happen. I should just go home now and forget this entire thing, because even if the embarrassment doesn't kill me, Jean-Mathias won't want me anymore when he meets his prospective in-laws.

He just peeked over my shoulder and told me nothing could make him not want me anymore. I knew there was a reason I love him. I need to stop overreacting and make plans. Jean-Mathias doesn't have any extra vacation, but I still have most of mine. I can take a week off and meet my parents in Paris, show them around there (something good can come from my visit there with Yves), and then bring them back to Grenoble for a few days so they can meet Jean-Mathias. And then take them back to Paris, maybe via Lyon, as soon as possible so they'll be safely back home.

I'll ask Mme Moreau for a recommendation for a hotel in town. I've never stayed in one since I'm always here or at Jean-Mathias's apartment. And of course Mom and Dad will want to meet her and M. Moreau. I think going out to dinner would be a good choice for that. Maybe… I don't know. I'll ask around and see if someone can suggest a good restaurant. There are probably hundreds of restaurants within the city and none of them bad, but I'd like to take them somewhere really nice, both as a way to say thank you to M. and Mme Moreau, since I don't really know how much longer I'll live here, and as a way to show my parents the best of what my new home has to offer.

Mom would probably scold me for being overly proud, but that's not really it. I want to give them a good impression of the life I'm building here: the country, the city, my job, and of course, Jean-Mathias. I want them to leave reassured that I'll be all right over here all by my lonesome. Not that I'll really be by my lonesome, not with Jean-Mathias and our friends, with Claude and Alexandre and the support from David et Jonathan. Another year or two and I'll probably not fit with the Pole Étudiant group anymore, but by then I may have found some other group, and even if I haven't, that's okay too. I have friends here, a job I like with a professor I respect. I have a lover who adores me and the feeling is mutual. I have everything I need to build a happy, solid life. I just have to help my parents see that.

Friday, February 28

I'm on the train on the way to Paris to meet Mom and Dad. My heart is pounding so hard it hurts, and I keep looking for Jean-Mathias for reassurance, but he isn't here. We talked about him coming with me today and spending the weekend before going back to work on Monday while I stay in Paris a couple days longer with Mom and Dad, but we ended up deciding it would be easier for them to have a few days with just me before they met him. That way I can talk to them in person and really make them understand how serious I am without any of us having to worry about holding back our words for the sake of public appearances. I love my parents, but I know how they are. If Jean-Mathias is there, they'll put on their company faces and everything will be polite, but it won't go any deeper than that.

That might be fine for company, but it won't work for the kind of conversations I need to have with them. I have ten days, and I need to send them home at the end of that time convinced I'm making, if not the right choice, at least an informed one. I know it's the right choice for me, but I may not ever convince them of <u>that</u>. At least I can try to convince them I've thought it through.

I decided against staying in the Marais. I don't want my parents shocked by being in the gay district and hostile because of it. We're staying in the seventh arrondissement near the Eiffel Tower. Nice and safe as far as their sensibilities are concerned.

I'll stay at the same hotel tonight and then if it isn't as nice as I think it is, I'll have a chance to look for something else tonight. They get in around eight thirty tomorrow, but they have to get their luggage and go through customs and immigration, so I told them I'd meet them at nine. We can take the train back into town, or get a cab if they want, and they can rest a little since I'll already have my hotel room. And then once they're ready to go, we can have lunch and get started on our visit.

I'm nervous. I shouldn't be nervous going to meet my parents, but I am. It's easy to say they can have whatever opinion they want, I'm doing this anyway. It's another thing entirely to face the fact that they may not accept this and if they don't, we may grow apart. Family has always been so important to me. I don't want to have to choose between my family and Jean-Mathias. I shouldn't have to choose between them. So why does it feel like I'm going to be forced to do just that?

Mom and Dad didn't say they were coming to talk sense into me. They didn't even imply it. They said they were coming to meet Jean-Mathias, and I want them to meet him. If we stay together like I hope we will, he'll be part of the family too, even if the realities of transatlantic flights keep us from seeing each other all that often. I'd want them to come for the ceremony. I'd want to take Jean-Mathias with me if I went home for a family event.

Yes, I know, I'm getting ahead of myself, but it <u>feels</u> right to think about these things, to think about him there with me at all the milestones of my life. And that means convincing Mom and Dad to accept him and us.

Maybe that's why I'm nervous. This is important in a way few things up until now have been.

We're pulling into the Gare de Lyon. Time to get my bag and find the hotel.

Saturday, March 1

I've retrieved Mom and Dad from the airport. They insisted they didn't want to nap, but they both wanted showers, so I'm taking a few minutes to write while they do that. I got a separate room for them, but they're using my shower now because it's too early to get into their room.

We decided to take a cab instead of the train back to the hotel. Mom and Dad look exhausted for all they say they don't want a nap, and I wasn't sure they were up to navigating the train system with their bags. The ride was a bit tense with everything I know they want to say but don't know how to, and all I want to say but didn't bring up so I wouldn't sound defensive. I think, though, that this is going to work because while it was tense, it wasn't hostile. We're going to have lunch at a little brasserie down the street, and then I'm going to take them to the Louvre if they feel up to it. And then maybe we can talk over dinner.

We had a long talk over dinner and after dinner. Mom and Dad are concerned about the distance, of course, and the cost of travel back and forth. I think they're a little bemused at my apparent abandonment of all things American in favor of all things French, although I tried to explain that wasn't the case at all, that I wasn't abandoning anything, but rather adding richness to my life. I don't think I convinced them. East Texas was always enough for them. I think they don't get why it isn't enough for me. The thing is, even if I went back to the US, I wouldn't go back home. To Houston or Dallas maybe, but not home. There isn't a job for me there, not to do medical research. I don't want to be a doctor. I want to be a researcher, and that requires a big hospital or research center and infrastructure. I tried telling them that, but I don't think it sank in. They're seeing it as a choice of me moving in down the street or staying in France. Even if I don't stay here, I could end up anywhere in the country except back at home.

They're a little worried I'm rushing into things with Jean-Mathias, and they don't believe me when I tell them staying another year to see what happens doesn't constitute rushing. I explained that my only other choice is to let it fizzle out because of distance. They didn't have an answer to that, but it doesn't seem to have convinced them either. I think the real problem is that the first they heard of Jean-Mathias was me telling them I was staying in France to be with him. That's my mistake, but there's nothing to be done about it now. I didn't tell them about him until I was sure there was something to tell, and by that time, I was already considering staying.

The only thing to do now is to keep talking and explaining and hope it eventually sinks in because I <u>am</u> staying next year and hopefully beyond that, and I'd like to do so with their blessing.

I should call Jean-Mathias. He'll want to know how the day went and he might have some suggestions for dealing with my parents that haven't occurred to me. And even if he doesn't, I'll feel better just from talking to him.

Sunday, March 2

Jean-Mathias and I talked for a long time last night. He didn't really have any suggestions, but simply talking to him made me feel better. Well, and phone sex.

If my parents ever read this, I'm <u>so</u> dead.

But, oh, damn, the things he said to me. The things he said he wanted to do to me and that he wanted me to do to him. I'm hard again just remembering it. I mean, some of it was stuff we've already done, like blowing each other, although we've never done it at the same time like he described, but some of it was stuff I can barely even get my mind around. His fingers, his mouth, his dick on my ass, in my ass. I can't decide if my ass is clenching because I want it or because I'm afraid of it. At one point talking to Claude, I said something about it being inevitable, not in the circumstances, but in my life. I'm a gay man, after all. He told me that wasn't true at all, that some guys never bottom, that some relationships don't include anal sex, and that's fine. It's like I said a couple of weeks ago. It's not how we touch each other, but why that matters. So I can take my time and think about it and even say no if I want, but knowing Jean-Mathias wants it will make it hard to resist. I've already learned that much about myself. He won't pressure me into anything, but I want to make him happy, and if that's what he wants, I know I'll end up doing it to make him happy. If I don't like it, I won't do it again, but at some point, at least once, I know we'll end up making love that way.

And honestly, as much as I don't see how it could be possible (big dick, little hole!), there's a part of me that wants to know what it would feel like, the ultimate in intimacy. I mean, seriously, can you get any closer than a guy's dick up your ass or vice versa?

Mom's knocking on my door saying they're ready for breakfast. How am I supposed to go out there with a hard-on? Ugh.

We had another wonderful day in Paris despite the rough start this morning. We walked to the Eiffel Tower and then across to the Arc de Triomphe and down the Champs-Élysées to the jardin des Tuileries. It was cold, but the sun was out and it felt good. I say it was cold. Mom and Dad kept talking about how cold it was, but it was still warmer than Grenoble. Jean-Mathias said it snowed there again last night, but it was above freezing here, by nearly ten degrees, so I enjoyed the warmth while they complained about the cold. Perspective is an amazing thing.

That's the crux of this entire visit. I have to get them to the point of seeing my life and my relationship with Jean-Mathias from my perspective. I understand their hesitations and concerns, but from where I'm standing, it's the most natural thing in the world to stay here and be with Jean-Mathias.

We head south tomorrow for a day in Lyon. We'll stay tomorrow night in Lyon and then go to Grenoble Tuesday morning. And Tuesday night, I get to introduce them to Jean-Mathias. Hopefully by then they'll at least have listened to me because if they start in on Jean-Mathias about how it would be better for him to let me go home, I'll lose it right then. There isn't any "letting" me do anything in this situation. I've told them I made this decision on my own, without Jean-Mathias even knowing about it until after I'd talked to Dr. Besson about the possibility of staying on.

Granted, if Jean-Mathias didn't feel the same way about me as I feel about him, I wouldn't stay, but he didn't ask me to stay. He isn't "keeping me here" as Mom keeps saying. I'm staying because this is where I want to be. And maybe that's splitting hairs, but I'm happy here. I like Grenoble, I like France, I like my job. I love Jean-Mathias.

This is what I want.

Tuesday, March 4

My parents really liked Lyon. I'm not surprised, actually. It's still a big city with all that entails, but it's smaller than Paris, more abordable, as the French would say. Approachable, I guess, or maybe accessible. They were much more relaxed as we visited Lyon than they were in Paris. Mom also said how proud she was of my French abilities, switching between French and English at need to talk to the conductor on the train or the people at the hotel or in restaurants. I don't think about it much anymore. I mean, I spend my days speaking nothing but French. It isn't anything special now. I just do it.

I guess that means I've hit fluency? If I don't think about it anymore?

Irrelevant.

I dropped my parents off at the hotel Mme Moreau recommended and came home to take a shower and change clothes. Jean-Mathias is picking me up at seven. We'll go back to the hotel to meet my parents and have dinner. It's probably petty of me to want to be with him instead of with them as they meet for the first time, but Jean-Mathias isn't some random person. He's my boyfriend. My lover. They have to deal with us as a couple. I won't be mean about it. I won't do anything overt to make them uncomfortable, but I won't let them isolate Jean-Mathias either, as if he were some interloper come to steal me away. I did that quite well on my own.

Tomorrow my parents are having dinner here with the Moreaus. Mme Moreau insisted they come to the house rather than us all going out to eat. Mom seemed really touched by that. I've reserved the hotel through Friday so we can go back to Paris and not have to worry about missing their flight out on Sunday. I'd like Jean-Mathias to come back with us, but I'm not sure how that would go over with my parents. It would probably be okay if we got separate hotel rooms, but that's expensive in Paris, not to mention it's giving in to a sense of propriety that doesn't apply here. We aren't some courting couple who needs to be kept separate until we get married. I can see Mom throwing her hands up in despair at my moral decay even as I write that, but it isn't about morals. Or maybe it is, but not in the way she wants to say. She wouldn't want us to live together or sleep together or do anything else together except maybe hold hands and kiss until we got married because that's what she did (or at least what she claims to have done. I'm having more and more trouble believing it, but that's a topic for a different entry). I love Jean-Mathias and he loves me. We want to begin building a life together. Okay, so it isn't marriage vows, but it _is_ a commitment and the beginning of our covenant. I'm not straight. I'm not going to have the big white wedding. I have to navigate the moral issues based on my reality, and I think I've done a damn fine job, even taking into consideration everything that happened with Yves.

Mom would probably disagree, but she isn't living my life. I have to do that myself, and I'm happy with the way it's turning out.

It's nearly seven. I should go so I won't keep Jean-Mathias waiting.

Dinner was both better and worse than I feared. Mom and Dad definitely got the message when Jean-Mathias and I arrived together. I could see Mom get that tightness around her lips that signals she isn't happy. She put on her company face, though, and shook Jean-Mathias's hand, complimenting him on how well he spoke English. (And he does. We'd never really talked about it before, but his English is very good, much better than my French was at the beginning of the year, for sure.) She asked him lots of polite questions about his job and his family and his career prospects. Not in those words, of course, but she definitely gave him the third degree.

And he charmed them both. He talked about his parents and the house in La Pérerrée, even offering to take them out to see it if they could stay in Grenoble an extra day and not go to Paris until Saturday evening. He told them his parents didn't speak a lot of English, but that they knew Mom and Dad were in town and had invited us out. He told my parents how much his parents had enjoyed meeting me, how they had invited me to Charles's birthday and how they always asked when I was going to come visit next. I didn't even know that part!

So we've changed our plans. We're going to La Pérerrée on Saturday morning and taking a late train to Paris Saturday night before my parents go home on Sunday.

I'm not entirely sure how I feel about that, but like Jean-Mathias said on the way back here tonight, if my parents see his parents embracing him, me, and us, maybe that will help Mom and Dad see that it can be done. And if it's a disaster, we'll deal with it.

On a completely unrelated note (actually probably not unrelated at all), I'm tired of leaving Jean-Mathias at night. I've already paid my rent to Mme Moreau for this month, but I think this will be my last month here. Unless Jean-Mathias can think of a reason to wait that hasn't occurred to me, I'm ready to take that step and move in with him. His apartment might be a little cramped with two of us, but it would be worth it not to watch him drive away every night.

I should get some sleep. My parents want to see Grenoble tomorrow, and I offered to take them skiing on Thursday.

Thursday, March 6

We've survived two more days. I've managed to get Mom to admit she can see why I like it here as we went around Grenoble yesterday. It's still mostly winter here, so the jardin de Ville and the other parks aren't interesting like they are in the summer, but the mountains are covered in snow, providing a stunning backdrop for the city. And we ate lunch at the café near work (they wanted to see where I work), so they got to meet Paolo. That helped them see I've started to develop a life here. I didn't go to David et Jonathan last night because they were here, but I told them about it. Not just that I usually go, but I talked to them about the group and the kinds of things we discuss and the attitude the people there have toward their faith and their sexuality.

It wasn't a comfortable conversation, but I think it helped them understand that I'm not walking away from everything they've taught me. I'm not rejecting them or my upbringing. I'm following the path laid out before me to the best of my ability and with the help of others who've had to deal with the same issues. I almost wish Mom and Dad spoke enough French to go with me to a meeting. It would do them a lot of good. Maybe not with me staying in France, but with my commitment to Jean-Mathias in more general terms.

We had a lovely dinner with the Moreaus last night. Serge and Elodie helped me play translator since M. and Mme Moreau's English is rusty and since my parents' French is nonexistent. Pierre wasn't there, but I didn't expect him to be. I still see him on Sundays sometimes if I'm home for dinner, but more weekends than not, I'm gone, out with Jean-Mathias or skiing or living my life. One more sign that the security I needed of having a family to stay with when I first got here isn't an issue anymore.

Skiing today was hilarious. Mom and Dad have never been skiing before and they aren't nearly as athletic in general as I am. We got lessons for them this morning so they could at least ski the green slopes without falling on their faces, but I'm not sure it's something they'll want to do again, even if they come visit in the winter. I stayed with them today rather than tackling some of the more challenging slopes. I can do that another weekend, after they leave. The season has another two months.

Jean-Mathias is going to let me borrow his car tomorrow so I can take Mom and Dad to Valence and down along the Rhône.

I don't know if they'll have any interest in any of the vineyards or wine tastings, but even if we don't stop there, both banks of the river are dotted with picturesque historic towns. And then Saturday, it's out to La Pérerrée. I'm still uncertain about the wisdom of that, but I'm not going to argue. It'll work or it'll be a disaster, but at least it'll be over.

Friday, March 7

To my surprise, we ended up doing some of the wine tastings today. Mom even bought a bottle to take home to the neighbor who's watching the house while they're gone. They're definitely softening their stance. I doubt they'll ever be happy about me staying here, but they are getting more comfortable with it. When we got back to Grenoble, Mom even suggested I call Jean-Mathias and invite him to join us for dinner since we didn't have other plans. I'm not sure how Dad felt about that, but he didn't stop me from making the call.

Jean-Mathias still got a handshake rather than a hug when we picked him up for dinner (since I had his car and all), but dinner tonight wasn't nearly as tense as dinner on Tuesday. After dinner, he dropped

Mom and Dad off at the hotel and offered to drive me home. I told him it was Friday and I saw no reason to change our routine just because my parents were in town. They were all safe and snug in their hotel. They wouldn't know where I slept and I wouldn't contradict them if they made an incorrect assumption.

So here I am sitting at the table in Jean-Mathias's apartment while he putters around. It's so incredibly domestic and it feels <u>so</u> right.

I'm moving in with Jean-Mathias at the end of the month. The words just sort of came out. I told him what I just wrote and he asked if there was any reason to wait any longer. I mentioned the rent I'd paid already, and he agreed I shouldn't ask for a refund on it, so I'll stay at the Moreaus, officially anyway, through the end of the month. But as of April 1, I will officially have a new address. I think I'll wait until March 31 to tell my parents, though. We've had a good visit and I don't want to spoil tomorrow's trip by telling them now and listening to them argue with me over it. Or yell at me because of it.

Maybe I'm selling them short, but I'd rather not take that chance, not with the trip to see the Pelissiers tomorrow.

Jean-Mathias is kissing my neck. I think that means it's time to put this away and go to bed.

Sunday, March 9

I got Mom and Dad on the plane and I'm on the train back to Grenoble. There wasn't really time to write last night, and I didn't want to write on the train on the way to Paris with them. It seemed like we should spend that time together.

The trip to La Pérerrée went reasonably well. The whole language barrier was more of an issue than it has been up until now. Jean-Mathias and I did our best to play translators, but there were lots of people there and I know my parents were overwhelmed at times. They hid it, but it's easy to get lost in a crowd when you're the only ones who don't speak the language.

Mme Pelissier (yes, I know, I'm supposed to call her Natalie) hugged me before we left to catch the train in Grenoble. I think that surprised Mom a bit. I think she expected Natalie to be in the same position she was in, still struggling to accept our relationship. Of course Natalie has had two months to get used to the idea, not that it took her that long, and Mom's only had a couple of weeks.

Dad still stopped with shaking Jean-Mathias's hand when he dropped us off at the train station, but Mom did hug him. It was an awkward hug, but it was a hug.

And this morning at the airport, when she hugged me good-bye, she whispered that she liked my young man. I'm not quite sure that's a blessing to stay in France and all the rest, but it's a start.

All in all, the trip hasn't gone nearly as badly as I was afraid it would. I'm sure I'll have to listen to the occasional question about when I'm coming home still, but I'll tell them when I'm coming to visit, the same as when I was in college. They dealt with it then. They can deal with it now.

It's back to work tomorrow and back to my regular routine. I also need to start thinking about what else I'll need to do if I'm going to stay here longer-term. Like maybe a French driver's license. Like buying a bike of my own. Getting a French credit card to go along with my debit card so I have the means to make bigger purchases.

I also should talk to Jean-Mathias about the rent and start looking at my budget and how the move will change that.

What else? I'm sure there's stuff I'm forgetting. I guess I can deal with it when I remember it or when it becomes obvious.

I'm really going to do this. I'm really going to stay in France. Um, wow.

I guess I should call Teresa. Now that Mom and Dad know, I need to tell everyone else, and she's definitely number one on the list of other people to tell. It's too early to call her now, and besides, I don't want to call from the train. It's rude and I never know when I'm going to lose cell service. I'll call her when I get back to Grenoble.

Saturday, March 15

When did Teresa get so hard to reach? I've been trying to call her since Sunday and just now got her on the phone. Of course part of that is time differences and stuff, and the fact that I didn't want to leave a message and panic her about why I was calling from France. So I told her I'd met someone and was going to stay on in France.

Her first reaction: Is he cute? I said yes. Her second reaction: When can I come visit? I told her she'd better wait until at least April since I didn't have a place for her to stay until I moved in with Jean-Mathias. I swear, her shriek damaged something in my ear. Then, of course, she wanted all the details. I left out the sex stuff. She doesn't need to hear that part. She wanted to hear it, but she doesn't need to hear it. Not that there's as much to tell her as she'd like to think there is, but that isn't the point. What Jean-Mathias and I do in bed is intensely personal and private and nobody's business but our own. I'm not ashamed of that expression of our love, but I don't want to share it either. Especially not now.

He fingered me last night. Not for long, but dear God, I've never felt anything like that. He was <u>inside</u> me. I could feel his finger sliding in and out, rubbing over this spot inside me, and oh, fuck, nothing we've done has felt so good. Not his hands on me, not his mouth on my dick. Nothing. And he promised that was only the start. I barely survived that. How am I going to survive more? Then later he kissed me and said he hoped someday I'd be ready to touch him the same way.

Somebody pinch me. I have to be dreaming. Not that I want to wake up, but I have to be dreaming. A year ago, thinking about my upcoming graduation, a part of me feared I'd always be alone because how could I reconcile my faith and my sexuality, how could I find someone who would respect both aspects of me, how could I live with the compromises I was sure walking this path would demand? And then I came here and met Claude and Alexandre, I met Jean-Mathias, and I started down this path. And I realized it isn't about compromising at all but about treating my relationship with Jean-Mathias with the same reverence and commitment God expects any married couple to show. It's about loving him enough to put him first and him loving me the same way.

And he does. He's so patient with my inexperience and my nerves and my need not to rush. He pays attention to what I need and what I want and gives them to me to the best of his ability. I never feel pressured or belittled because of my virginity or my faith. I will say I'm glad one of us knows what he's doing. It never would have occurred to me to get some kind of lubrication, but I have a feeling it would have hurt without it. At the same time, he doesn't lord that experience over me. He doesn't make me wonder if something's wrong with me, that I'm twenty-two (twenty-three next week!) and haven't done this before. He makes me feel like my trust is a gift he's striving to be worthy of.

He's worthy of it. In a way I wish he could have been my first everything. My first kiss, my first touch, my only lover in any sense of the word, but I learned from those relationships. I learned I was better off with Jean-Mathias, but maybe I needed those experiences to open my eyes to what was right in front of me. He certainly doesn't seem to begrudge me my mistakes.

Friday, March 21

Happy birthday to me!

I have no idea what Jean-Mathias has planned for tonight, but he made me promise to let him arrange everything. How could I say no to that? So all I know is I'm supposed to pack a bag for the weekend, including at least one outfit for going out, and to be ready to leave from work. I've got my bag packed (with two nice outfits just in case), and I'm leaving for work in a few minutes.

Jean-Mathias just told me if I wanted to write in my journal tonight, I'd better do it now because he planned on leaving me so boneless when he was done with me that I wouldn't want to get up before noon tomorrow.

He took me out to dinner tonight for my birthday to l'Auberge Napoléon. It's not the most expensive restaurant in Grenoble, but it is supposed to be one of the best. It certainly was delicious. You can just tell when everything's fresh. With the temperatures finally rising a little, we went for a walk along the river after dinner and then through the old part of town. All in all, a very romantic evening. Now we're back at his apartment (soon to be our apartment!) with a bottle of wine and the evening to ourselves. And it looks like my writing time is up. I'll write more tomorrow.

Saturday, March 22

It's one o'clock in the afternoon. I didn't wake up until half an hour ago. I'd say Jean-Mathias kept his promise. Damn, did he keep his promise! I think the term is rimming, but whatever the word for it, I came and came and came for what felt like hours.

I know, that isn't physically possible. Screw that. He put his mouth on me and I lost it and didn't stop until he did. And he didn't stop for a long, long time.

I thought having his fingers inside me was intimate, but that was nothing (okay, maybe not nothing, but you know what I mean) compared to having his tongue inside me.

It feels stupid to say I never really thought about it, but it's not like I've read or watched a lot of porn or had a lot of experience, and I only started wrapping my head around the whole gay thing eighteen months ago or so, during my final year of college, so this is all still new to me. I "got" the whole blow job idea even when I wasn't comfortable doing it, but there's a part of me that keeps thinking he can't possibly have put his mouth there. But he did and it felt so hot and illicit and like we shouldn't have been doing it, but it was too amazing to stop, and he licked and sucked and pushed inside me and I couldn't breathe for the sheer overpowering need of it all. I still can't breathe when I think about it. His hair brushing my legs and then my balls as he buried his face in my ass and just stayed there. And then rolling over for him to make it easier, on my knees with him behind me. It felt so dirty and so right at the same time. I don't even want to think what I must have sounded like, begging him not to stop, but he obviously didn't mind because he didn't tell me to shut up and he sure didn't stop. Not until the sheets were soaked. We slept on the bare mattress last night because the sheet was too much of a mess and we didn't have the energy to put on a clean sheet.

Or at least I didn't have the energy to get up so he could put on a clean sheet. He might have been fine. I was so gone by the time he finally stopped making love to me that I didn't even check on him. Talk about selfish. I'll have to find a way to make it up to him later. I don't think I'm ready to return last night's favor, but I can come up with some way to show him I appreciate his attention.

First, though, I should take a shower and see if he has plans for today. If he doesn't, I know what my plans are. Seeing how quickly I can drag him back to bed.

Jean-Mathias had other plans for today. We're in La Pérerrée. His family threw a surprise birthday party for me. Romain and Xavier were there, along with all of Jean-Mathias's family. Natalie said since I couldn't be with my family for my birthday, she thought I should have the next closest thing.

I was so touched. She's right too. If I'm going to stay here in France with Jean-Mathias, if we decide to form a PACS down the road, or honestly even if we don't, I'll be Natalie and François's son-in-law. I hadn't really thought in those terms until today, but it's clear they've started thinking in those terms. I assume Jean-Mathias told them we're moving in together. Natalie certainly seemed to know although I didn't hear Jean-Mathias tell her. Then again, he probably called her sometime over the last month. It's not like we just decided yesterday.

Of course this means I didn't get to drag him back to bed, and while we'll share Jean-Mathias's room tonight because Xavier and Romain are crashing in Edwige's room where I slept the last time we were here overnight, I'm not entirely comfortable jumping Jean-Mathias in his parents' house. I wonder if I can stay at his apartment again tomorrow night and go home after work on Monday. I'm only going to be living at the Moreaus for another week. I should probably start moving some of my stuff anyway, just so it's easier next weekend. So if I stay tomorrow night and leave what I already have at his apartment, I can take the empty bag home Monday afternoon and bring another load over. And I can make love to Jean-Mathias in our bed tomorrow night.

Sunday, March 23

Or apparently I can make love with him in his bed in La Pérerrée. He assured me the walls were thick enough and the rooms distant enough that his parents wouldn't hear us as long as we didn't make too much noise, and then he made me scream. If Natalie and François heard us, they didn't say anything this morning, fortunately. I don't think I could have lived with the embarrassment. I mean, okay, we're moving in together. They have to assume we're having sex, but there's a difference between assuming and having it rubbed in your face. Romain smirked at me this morning, but he left it at that, so I'm guessing the walls aren't as thick as Jean-Mathias thinks they are.

And I'm not very good at staying quiet. Not when Jean-Mathias puts his hands and mouth on me.

I really am going to steal control from him tonight and return the favor. I haven't told him that yet, but I'm determined. Tonight he gets to lie back and come screaming while I tease and torment him for hours.

Monday, March 24

I realize experience is the only cure for inexperience, but I could really deal with being past the whole awkward, "don't know what I'm doing" stage of making love. As we were getting ready for bed last night, I told Jean-Mathias I wanted to make love to him instead of lying back and making him do all the work. I honestly expected him to hesitate or refuse, or at least try to cajole me out of it, but he didn't. He kissed me and told me he was all mine to do whatever I wanted with. Those may well be the sexiest words I've ever heard because they mean he trusts me implicitly.

Everything started out okay. I mean, we've gotten pretty comfortable with each other and I've gotten better at some things. I can give a decent hand job, and Jean-Mathias has never complained about anything else either, but I'm definitely not used to being the one to decide what to do next.

Jean-Mathias was as good as his word, lying back and letting me touch him however I wanted without trying to take over, and from the sounds he was making, I managed to make him feel good. That didn't keep me from feeling like I was floundering, though. He came while I was sucking on his balls, but I was so nervous I wasn't even close. Not exactly fun, sexy times.

I apologized to Jean-Mathias. He pointed out the wet spot on the sheet and assured me that however ill at ease I felt, he felt loved.

That totally ended the argument and made me feel a lot better. Yes, I felt incredibly awkward, but I obviously didn't do it "wrong" because I made him feel good. I guess the trick here is to do it more often, so I don't feel like I'm fumbling all the time. There's a certain appeal to that thought.

Thursday, March 27

My last night at the Moreaus' house. As excited as I am about moving in with Jean-Mathias and beginning our life together, it's a little sad to leave. I've enjoyed working with Serge and Elodie on their English. I've enjoyed the family dinners and the conversations and just being here. It's not like I can't still see them. I'm moving out of their house, not out of town or out of the country.

I filed a change of address form at work today, which means I have some other paperwork to file too, apparently, but I'll deal with all of that tomorrow and next week. Mme Moreau said I should come by every few days for a while to make sure I got my mail. I can't do an address change at the post office because the whole household isn't moving, just me.

My bags are all packed. I've moved half my stuff over the course of the week already, so it's just a question of tossing in the last minute things tomorrow morning and then picking up my bags after work. How have I accumulated so much stuff? I've only been here for, okay, fine, for nine months. I guess that's how I've accumulated so much stuff. Jean-Mathias is going to change his mind about letting me move in when I start trying to unpack and put my stuff in his little apartment.

Our little apartment.

I seem to have no problem thinking of our bed, but I can't quite get my head around our apartment. Not quite sure why that is. When I start helping to clean the toilet or pay the rent, I'm sure it'll start feeling like mine.

It's getting late. I should go to bed. Tomorrow is a big day.

Saturday, March 29

So you know how I said yesterday would be a big day. It was, even more than I expected. I knew it was moving day, commitment day in a small sense. I didn't expect it to be the day I lost my virginity.

Not that I'm complaining! God, no, I'm not complaining! I just wasn't expecting it. I mean, I didn't expect to stay a virgin forever, and I didn't really expect even to wait for a PACS, but somehow I didn't think it would happen last night. I probably should have thought about it, given that I was already thinking about how much of a commitment it was for us to move in together.

So anyway, last night.

Yeah, um.

Why is it I can write about blow jobs and rimming and I can't seem to put the words on paper to describe last night?

I know there are words. Romance novelists use them all the time, but they aren't my words and this isn't a romance novel. It is, however, my journal, specifically my journal of coming to terms with myself as a gay man, and last night was part of that. A huge part of it. Because even with everything else Jean-Mathias and I have done together, all the lovemaking, last night, having his dick inside me, was different. I don't know how to explain it exactly. I mean, there shouldn't be all that much difference between having his fingers in me and his dick in me, but there is.

There's a difference on a physical level because of size, but that's not what I'm talking about. It's the sense of connection, of having his body completely covering mine, joined with mine, so we aren't two bodies anymore, but one being, one complete entity, a circle that goes round and round and round but never ends.

Okay, so maybe I'm a little more romantic than I thought I was.

And maybe it's juvenile to equate penetrative sex with a long-term commitment, but that's the way I was raised, and everything about last night felt like that's what it was. Jean-Mathias drove me over to the Moreaus' after work so we could get the rest of my stuff, and then we came back here and brought everything inside. I unpacked a bit while he cooked. Something I'll have to learn, I guess. Either that or I can offer to always do the dishes if he'll keep cooking. Anyway, we ate dinner together in our apartment. No fanfare, just the beginning of a life together. There was a movie on TV Jean-Mathias wanted to watch, so we moved to the living room and watched that for a while, snuggled together, his arm around my shoulders, my head on his shoulder. Comfortable. Right.

The movie ended and Jean-Mathias got up and said something about it being late and we should go to bed. I didn't think anything of it. I mean, I live here now. Obviously we're going to bed at some point.

We got ready for bed like usual, taking turns in the bathroom to brush our teeth and everything. A comfortable routine of togetherness.

Jean-Mathias was already in bed when I came out of the bathroom, so I got undressed and climbed in bed with him, thinking we'd get each other off and then get some sleep. It took all of about thirty seconds to realize he had other plans.

I have never felt more adored than he made me feel last night, his hands and lips on my body, using everything he's learned about me over the last three months to reduce me to a puddle. When he'd rimmed and fingered me until I thought I couldn't stand it anymore, he stroked my face and asked if he could be inside me, and I thought I'd never heard anything more perfect in my life.

Then I felt him pressing against me, all hot and slick and big, but I needed him so much by then that I didn't care that it stung. He was so patient with me, letting me adjust so it never went from a bit of a sting to actual pain. And finally he was inside me, lying fully on top of me, as close as two people can be. When he started moving, his dick hitting my prostate with every pass, I couldn't stop myself. It felt like every hit was another little mini-orgasm that built and built and built and when it was done, I really was a puddle of goo on the bed.

Of course, he was a puddle of goo inside and on top of me, so at least I wasn't the only one affected.

It's kind of odd to be sitting here writing this entry. It feels like the story has come to an end, like the chapter of my life this journal was meant to record is over. I'm out. I'm not flaming, but I'm proud. I've met my lover. I know there's still a journey ahead of us, the one of our life together, but that's a different story. One I'm looking forward to living.

Friday, March 27

I found this today as Jean-Mathias and I were putting the final things in boxes to move to our new apartment when we get back. I can't believe I haven't written in it for a year. I'd promise to do better except I think what I wrote at the end of the last entry is right. The story we're living now is a different one, for a different journal if I ever decide to write it.

This entry is a footnote really, so if anyone else ever finds this and reads it, they'll know how it all turned out. We're going to the Mairie tomorrow to make our PACS, and then we leave for a week in Martinique for our honeymoon.

I wanted us to get married on the anniversary of the day we moved in together, but that's a Sunday so the mayor's office is closed. Jean-Mathias, wonderful man that he is, told me it was close enough and that it didn't have to be the exact day for it to mean everything to him.

If possible, I've fallen more in love with him than I was a year ago. I wouldn't have believed it then, but it makes me hopeful for the years ahead.

Mom and Dad are here for the ceremony. They're staying with Natalie and François, who have definitely become my parents as well. Mom even started taking French lessons so she can talk to them better. Not great, but definitely better than last year when they came to visit.

I started this journal by thinking about my once-in-a-lifetime experience, but it isn't a once-in-a-lifetime thing at all. It's a once-for-my-lifetime experience, and that's a far, far more precious thing.

Time to put this away. My lover is calling.

ARIEL TACHNA lives outside of Houston with her husband, her daughter and son, and their cat. Before moving there, she traveled all over the world, having fallen in love with both France, where she found her husband, and India, where she dreams of retiring some day. She's bilingual with snippets of four other languages to her credit and is as in love with languages as she is with writing.

Visit Ariel's web site at http://www.arieltachna.com/ and her blog at http://arieltachna.livejournal.com/.

Contemporary Romance by ARIEL TACHNA

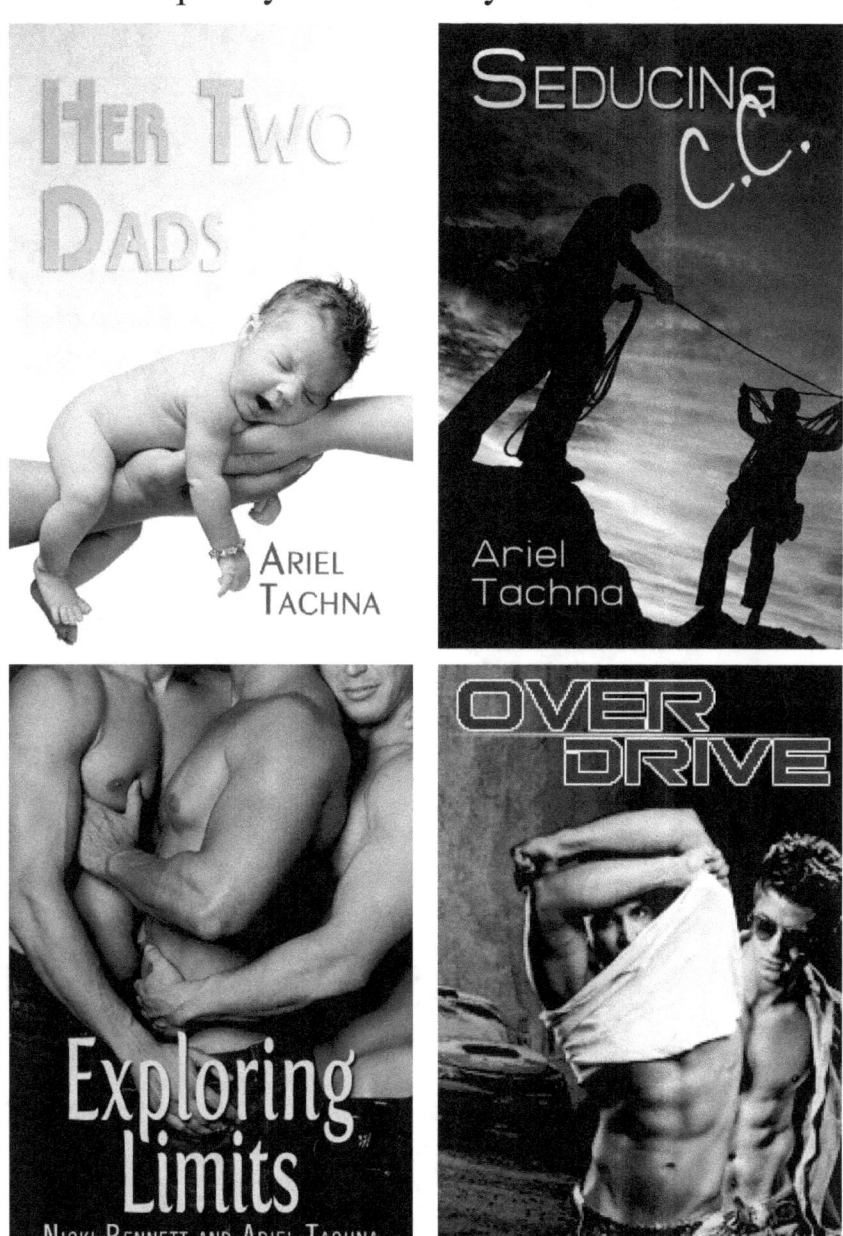

Also by ARIEL TACHNA

http://www.dreamspinnerpress.com

Historical Romance by ARIEL TACHNA

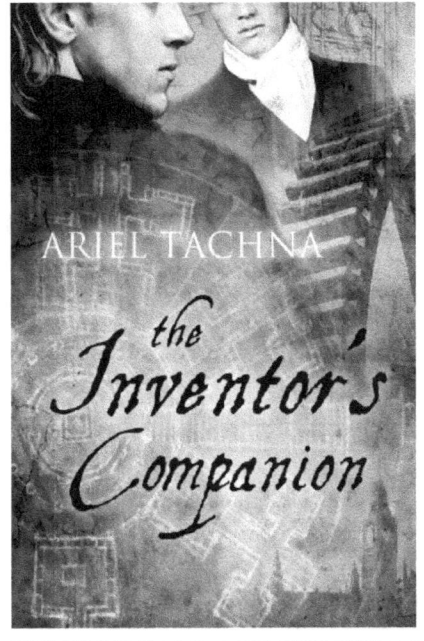